SISTER THE VAMPIRE

FANGTASTIC!

HAMILTON COLLEGE LIBRARY

Sink your fangs into these:

Switched

Revamped!

Vampalicious

HAMILTON COLLEGE LIBRARY

Sienna Mercer

MY SISTER THE VAMPIRE

FANGTASTIC!

EGMONT

With special thanks to Josh Greenhut

For Jenny Meyer, who totally sucks

EGMONT
We bring stories to life

My Sister the Vampire: Fangtastic! first published in Great Britain 2009
by Egmont UK Limited
239 Kensington High Street
London W8 6SA

Copyright © Working Partners Ltd 2009
Created by Working Partners Limited, London WC1X 9HH

ISBN 978 1 4052 4370 4

9 10 8

A CIP catalogue record for this title is available from the British Library

Typeset by Avon DataSet Ltd, Bidford on Avon, Warwickshire
Printed and bound in Great Britain by the CPI Group

All rights reserved. No part of this publication may be reproduced,
stored in a retrieval system, or transmitted, in any form or by any means,
electronic, mechanical, photocopying, recording or otherwise, without
the prior permission of the publisher and copyright owner.

Chapter One

Ivy Vega trudged sleepily into the breakfast room, slid into her chair, and rested her cheek on the cool stone table. She wished she was still in her coffin. Monday mornings were the worst.

'Good morning, sleepybones,' her father said, placing a bowl next to her head.

'Shh,' Ivy murmured, her eyes closed. 'I'm still sleeping.'

'It's your favourite,' her dad coaxed. 'Marshmallow Platelets.'

Ivy peered at the little white marshmallows

bobbing in their milky sea of maroon bits. 'Thanks,' she mumbled.

Her father, already dressed for work in black chinos and a black pinstriped shirt with French cuffs, sipped his tea and picked up the remote control. 'There is nothing better for a young person's dull morning mind,' he said, 'than dull morning television.'

He flipped through the weather and some talk shows before settling on *The Morning Star*.

'Please, no,' Ivy said. 'Just looking at Serena Star's smile gives me sunburn.'

Serena Star, WowTV's best celebrity reporter, had impossibly bright, dyed blonde hair and eyes that looked as if they'd been surgically enhanced to be permanently wide open in either adoration or shock. Lately, she'd been trying to cast herself as a serious journalist on her own morning news show, *The Morning Star*. Just the other day, Ivy had turned the TV off in exasperation after Serena had said, 'Tell me, Mr Senator, how does it feel to have a law named after you?'

This morning, Serena Star was standing with her back to a small crowd of people, talking into her microphone. She was wearing a tiny blue suede miniskirt under a knee-length trench coat, and the look in her wide eyes said 'shock!'. She was in a park, or maybe a graveyard. A scruffy, black-clad teenager stood beside her –

Ivy's dad flipped the channel.

'Turn back!' Ivy blurted.

'But you said –'

'I know. Turn back!' she repeated.

Ivy could not believe her eyes. The boy standing next to Serena Star was none other than Garrick Stephens, one of the lamest vampires at her school. He and his bonehead friends – everyone called them the Beasts – were always pulling dumb stunts, like seeing which one of them could eat the most garlic croutons without getting seriously ill. They weren't nearly as scary as they smelled, but they'd been annoying since forever.

What is he doing on national TV? Ivy wondered.

'I think that's the local cemetery,' her dad said.

Ivy realised he was right – this was being filmed less than five blocks from their house.

The camera panned over to an empty grave and Ivy's dad turned up the volume.

'. . . yesterday's small-town funeral went horribly wrong,' Serena Star was saying off-screen. 'Local deceased man, Mr Alan Koontz, was scheduled for burial here at the Franklin Grove Memorial Cemetery. As Mr Koontz was being lowered into the ground, eyewitnesses say that his casket creaked open.' The camera zoomed in on a shiny midnight-blue coffin lying open next to the grave. 'In a bizarre turn of events, out climbed an allegedly *live* person!' Serena continued. 'Mr Koontz's widow immediately fainted, and was rushed to Franklin Grove General Hospital for treatment.'

Serena Star's frowning face reappeared on the screen. 'Friends of the family say that the person who emerged bore no resemblance to Mr Koontz and was, in fact, a teenaged boy.' The camera pulled back to reveal Garrick, who was licking his palm and using it to slick back his hair.

Ivy was frowning now too; Garrick and his friends didn't know the meaning of the word 'discreet'. They probably couldn't even spell it. Since they were little kids, Ivy had always been amazed at how close the Beasts routinely came to breaking the First Law of the Night: vampires are *never* supposed to reveal their true selves to an outsider.

Thinking about that made Ivy feel uncomfortable. After all, she'd recently broken the First Law herself. She'd had no choice, though: she couldn't possibly keep the fact that she was a vampire secret from her identical twin, Olivia, even if Olivia was human.

She and Olivia had only discovered each other at the beginning of the school year. They'd been separated at birth and adopted by different parents, so Ivy hadn't known that she had a twin until Olivia turned up at Franklin Grove Middle. And it had been just as great a shock to Olivia.

I may have broken the First Law, but at least I didn't reveal myself to the whole world on national TV! Ivy thought.

Serena Star looked squarely at the camera. 'I, Serena Star, now bring you an exclusive interview with the thirteen-year-old boy who was almost buried alive. I think you'll agree it's a story that's truly . . . INDEADIBLE!' A graphic with the word 'INDEADIBLE!' materialised on the screen over Garrick's head, and Ivy rolled her eyes. Serena was always making up lame words for her on-screen headlines.

'Awesome!' Garrick Stephens grinned.

Ivy's head ached. *How in the underworld*, she thought, *are we going to cover up a vampire popping out of a coffin in the middle of a funeral?*

'Mr Stephens.' Serena Star turned to face her subject. 'How do you feel?'

'I feel great!' Garrick said.

'Amazing!' Serena commented, with a slight frown. She had clearly been expecting Garrick to be upset. 'How long were you in that coffin?'

'Like seven, eight hours.'

'That must have been very unsettling,' Serena Star prompted sympathetically.

'Only when those pallbearer guys carried it

around and woke me up,' Garrick said, shooting a peeved look off-camera.

'Are you saying you were asleep in there?' asked Serena Star, her wide eyes widening even further.

'Yeah,' Garrick answered. 'I slept like I was dead.'

Ivy winced as Serena Star shook her head in disbelief. 'You almost sound like you enjoyed yourself.'

Garrick shrugged.

'Mr Stephens,' Serena Star said, a hint of disapproval in her voice, 'what kind of person sleeps in a coffin?'

'It wasn't my idea,' Garrick shrugged.

'Oh?' said Serena Star. 'Whose idea was it?'

Garrick was about to answer, but then he seemed to think better of it. He crossed his arms. 'I don't want to get them into trouble.'

'Are you saying the people who did this to you are *friends* of yours?' Serena Star asked.

'Totally,' Garrick replied, grinning.

'You mean –'

'We're the kings of Franklin Grove Middle!' Garrick cried, mugging wildly. 'Yo, Kyle, Ricky, Dylan! I'm on TV!'

What an utter dork! thought Ivy.

'What exactly did your friends have in mind?' Serena Star probed.

'They dared me to climb in,' Garrick explained, his eyes glinting mischievously. 'That's why I did it.'

Ivy could tell Garrick was lying from the smug look on his face. He was just pretending it was a dare to avoid revealing any vampire secrets – like the fact that we sleep in coffins. Still, it was a pretty lame alibi, especially because he kept going on about how it was 'the best sleep' of his life.

'The Interna 3 is the sweetest coffin ever,' he gushed, grabbing the microphone. 'When they say "rest in peace", they mean it!'

'Mr Stephens, please,' Serena interrupted. 'That still doesn't explain how you ended up at Mr Koontz's funeral.'

'Oh, right. My friends just sort of thought it would be funny to leave me in there – thanks a lot guys!' Garrick winked. 'Then the funeral home got the coffins mixed up. Did you know the Interna 3 is the best-selling coffin in America?'

Serena Star yanked the microphone away. 'Are we to believe that this was really just an innocent student prank?' she said to Garrick, who shrugged.

'Or,' she continued, turning slowly to the camera, 'is there something *more sinister* at work?'

Uh-oh. Ivy thought. *Serena Star smells blood.*

'Clearly, a gruesome obsession with death,'

Serena went on as the camera zoomed in for a close-up of her shocked face, 'nearly cost this misguided young misfit his life!'

'Who are you calling misguided?' Garrick's voice whined off-screen.

'And he isn't alone,' Serena said, ignoring Garrick. 'One look around this sleepy town reveals a dark obsession consuming the minds of its children.' The live feed cut briefly to footage of the mall, showing a group of Goth sixth-graders.

'Are the youth of America next?' Serena asked, ominously, as she reappeared on screen. Then she frowned with determination. 'I, Serena Star, will not rest until I find out the evil truth behind what's happening here.'

Oh no, Ivy thought. *She's going to say that line of hers.*

'Because the Star of truth must shine!' Serena Star declared dramatically, pumping her microphone in the air. It really was the worst journalistic sign-off Ivy had ever heard. 'This is Serena Star. Wake up, America!'

A commercial came on, and Ivy's dad shut off the TV. 'You must promise me,' he said, 'that if you are ever on television, you will make a better impression than that boy, Garrick Stephens.'

'It's not funny, Dad,' Ivy said. 'If Serena Star starts seriously investigating Goths in Franklin Grove, you know what she might find. What if she scoops the existence of vampires? None of us will ever be safe again!'

Her father put down his tea. 'Ivy,' he said, 'we are talking about a woman best known for her special exposé on the footwear of the rich and famous! I very much doubt she's capable of finding any real proof. Besides, the moment there's a new bit of Hollywood gossip, Serena Star will forget all about Franklin Grove.'

Ivy sighed. 'I hope you're right,' she said, standing up to take her empty bowl into the kitchen, 'because if not, it's going to be really hard to get Marshmallow Platelets around here.'

🦇   🦇   🦇

As they pulled up in front of Franklin Grove Middle on Monday morning, Olivia Abbott was applying her pink lipstick in the visor mirror when she heard her mother gasp. Olivia flipped up the visor to see the front steps of the school packed with people, and a string of TV news vans lining the kerb.

'Wow!' said Olivia.

Her mother double-parked and started to get out of the car.

Olivia grabbed her mom's arm. 'Where are you going?'

'I want to see what all the commotion's about,' her mother replied.

Olivia shook her head. 'You can't come with me into school.'

'Why not?' her mother asked.

'Because I'm in eighth grade,' Olivia explained.

Olivia's mom smiled and shook her head. 'Well, OK,' she sighed.

'It's not you,' Olivia assured her. 'It's all mothers. It's like a rule. I'll call you.' And, with that, Olivia pecked her mom on the cheek, climbed out of the car, and squeezed between two news vans.

She started up the steps, trying not to trip on any of the TV crews' electrical cords as she weaved through the people. Scanning the reporter-studded crowd, she spotted a flash of soft blonde curls up ahead. 'Camilla!' she called.

Camilla Edmunson turned and waved. When Olivia joined her, Camilla said, 'Can you believe this?'

'What's going on?' asked Olivia.

'Everyone's trying to get on TV,' Camilla answered. Nearby, Olivia saw Kyle Glass, one of the group of boys everyone called the Beasts, holding up a pair of fingers to look like bunny ears behind an unsuspecting reporter's head. The cameraman was waving frantically in an attempt to shoo him away.

Olivia frowned. 'Uh, did I miss something?'

'You mean you haven't heard?' Camilla asked incredulously. 'Garrick Stephens popped out of a coffin in the middle of someone's funeral yesterday. It was like when the villain Zolten escaped by hiding in a cryopod.'

Olivia assumed her friend was referring to one of the sci-fi books she loved. Olivia herself had always been more into vampire fiction. In fact, when she'd moved to Franklin Grove, she'd thought that vampires were *only* fiction.

Boy, had she been wrong. She still got dizzy when she stopped to think about the fact that Franklin Grove was teeming with living, breathing, blood-sipping vampires. Most of them, Garrick and his friends excluded, were really nice.

None of the other humans in Franklin Grove had any inkling that their town was like Vamp Central, because that was the Number One Biggest Rule of Vampiredom: *no telling*. So popping out of a coffin during a funeral was probably off-limits.

The only reason Olivia knew about the vampires was because of Ivy Vega, who she'd met on her first day at Franklin Grove Middle. Olivia was pure cheerleader and Ivy was uber-Goth, so at first they had seemed as different as black licorice and cotton candy. But it hadn't taken long for Olivia and Ivy to realise that they looked *exactly* alike.

In fact – and this is where, Olivia thought, it gets really mind-blowing – they were identical twins. Identical that is, except for one thing: Ivy was a vampire!

'Anyway,' Camilla was saying, 'the whole of America is now fascinated by Franklin Grove, and the media – especially Serena Star – is trying to turn Garrick into this huge story about the decline of America's youth.'

'No way.' Olivia's jaw dropped. 'Serena Star from WowTV? She's totally famous!'

Camilla nodded, but she clearly wasn't as impressed. 'She thinks we're all hiding some terrible secret.'

Olivia's heart skipped a beat. 'Like what?'

'Who knows?' said Camilla. 'It's not like she's going to find anything. Franklin Grove is probably the most normal town in America.'

Olivia smiled uncomfortably. Camilla didn't have a clue.

I'd better find Ivy, Olivia thought, *and see what she has to say about all this!* 'Wanna go in?' she asked.

She and Camilla skirted the crowd on their way to the front doors of the school. Suddenly, Olivia heard a familiar high-pitched voice call her name. She tried to ignore it and keep walking, but the voice shrieked even louder: 'OLIVIA!'

Olivia winced and told Camilla to go on without her. Then she reluctantly turned to see Charlotte Brown, her cheerleading captain, gesturing for Olivia to join her in a circle of cameras.

Ever since Olivia had made the squad a few weeks ago, it was as if Charlotte had forgotten that she'd tried to sabotage Olivia at tryouts. In fact, Charlotte and her friends Katie and Allison all treated Olivia like she was their BFF. *At least it keeps the squad cheering as a team*, Olivia thought as she made her way over.

'Tell them, Olivia!' Charlotte said, grabbing her arm and pulling her in front of the cameras. 'You know – what it's like as a new student here. How frightening it is with all the bad influences.'

Olivia scrunched her nose. A camera flashed. 'I, uh, don't really –'

A reporter in a rumpled suit stuck a microphone in front of Olivia's face. 'Have you ever slept in a coffin?'

'No,' Olivia said incredulously.

A woman holding a tape recorder asked, 'Are you familiar with a street gang known as the Beasts?'

Olivia shook her head. 'I wouldn't exactly call them –'

A short, determined-looking woman in a tight, bright orange suit muscled in between the others, her blonde hair shining in the sun. Olivia gasped; it was Serena Star herself! She looked much shorter than she did on TV.

'Have you ever,' Serena Star said, thrusting her microphone under Olivia's chin, 'felt threatened by everyone around you wearing black?'

What a silly question! thought Olivia. 'Since when is there anything wrong with wearing black?' she asked.

Charlotte leapt in front of her. 'Yes, Ms Star, I totally have!' she cried, clearly overexcited to be talking to a celebrity reporter like Serena. 'Once,' she said, flipping her hair dramatically, 'I was in the girls' bathroom, re-applying gloss, when two Goth girls came in. They were dressed from head to toe in black rags, and their nails were covered in black nail polish. And guess what they did. They *growled* at me!'

'Growled at you?' Serena Star repeated.

'Uh huh,' Charlotte nodded seriously. 'I was so scared I ran out without even doing my mascara!'

'So you think it's a problem,' Serena Star pressed, 'that so many Franklin Grove students are obsessed with darkness?'

'Totally!' Charlotte agreed. 'Black is so last season.' She gestured towards Serena Star's turquoise stiletto heels. 'I absolutely *love* your shoes by the way. Are they from Hollywood?'

Olivia seized the opportunity to slip away, racing up the steps and through the school's front doors. She had to talk to her twin about what was going on outside.

From down the hall, she spotted Ivy standing by her locker with her new boyfriend, Brendan Daniels. Even Brendan had yet to notice that she and Ivy looked alike. 'See you later, OK?' Olivia heard Brendan say.

Ivy twirled the emerald ring hanging around

her neck. 'OK,' she cooed. Her sister was still *so* smitten. Olivia thought it was super-cute.

As she waited for Ivy and Brendan to finish their goodbyes, Olivia played with the ring on her finger. It was actually their matching emerald rings that had helped Ivy and Olivia recognise each other. The rings were all either of them had from their birth parents.

Brendan walked by with a friendly, 'Hey, Olivia!' and Olivia scooted up to her sister.

'Let me guess,' Olivia began. 'You still haven't told him about us.'

'I swear I've tried,' Ivy answered, pulling off a sheer black sweater to reveal a grey baby tee with an illustration of Edgar Allen Poe's face on it. 'But it never seems like the right moment to say, "Hey, by the way, I have a twin sister I never knew about."'

'Eventually,' said Olivia, 'we're going to have

to tell everyone, including our parents.'

Suddenly there was a commotion down the hall, and Olivia looked up to see Garrick Stephens strolling along in sunglasses and a black T-shirt that said *INTERNA 3 – REST IN PEACE!* The other Beasts were trailing behind him. People were parting to let them through, like Garrick was a star quarterback who had just won a big game – or else a quarterback who had just lost the big game by running into the wrong end zone. 'Autographs?' Garrick called nonchalantly. 'Autographs?'

Ivy shook her head angrily. 'I'm going to strangle him,' she said. 'Can you believe I had to come in the side door this morning? Brendan did, too. Otherwise we never would have made it up the front steps alive.'

'That's what I wanted to talk to you about,' Olivia replied. 'I saw Charlotte being interviewed by Serena Star. She said two Goths once growled at her in the bathroom.'

'That wasn't a growl,' Ivy protested. 'That was a bark. For night's sake, she got a perm last year that made her look like a poodle.'

Olivia laughed, but her sister turned serious.

'This is really grave, Olivia,' Ivy said anxiously. 'I thought maybe the story would just go away quietly, but that's not going to happen with all these reporters hanging around, and people like Charlotte and Garrick jockeying for the spotlight.'

Sophia Hewitt, Ivy's oldest friend, appeared, her big digital camera hanging around her neck. 'Code black,' she whispered cryptically. 'I repeat, code black.' And, with that, she disappeared down the hall.

Ivy rushed to pull her black leather bag on to her shoulder and slammed her locker shut.

'What's code black?' Olivia asked in a low voice.

'Science hall bathroom,' Ivy said, taking off down the hall. Olivia hurried to keep up.

The two of them pushed through the bathroom door to find Sophia checking underneath the stalls to make sure the bathroom was deserted.

Then she spun around to face Ivy and Olivia with her hands on her hips. 'Garrick Stephens wasn't on a dare. He was window shopping!'

'Are you serious?' Ivy asked.

'Dead serious,' replied Sophia.

Olivia said, 'I don't get it.'

'Vamps upgrade their coffins like most people upgrade cell phones,' Ivy explained.

'And the Interna 3 is the latest, greatest dreambox of all,' Sophia added. 'It's not like Garrick could afford it. He just thought it would be fun to try it.'

Ivy frowned. 'Funeral homes are often run by

25

vampires. Their showrooms are multi-purpose. But this time they must have gotten the showroom coffin mixed up with the dead guy's.'

Sophia bit one black fingernail. 'I'm really worried, Ivy. Serena Star seems desperate for a big story. Even if she can't find one, she'll probably just make one up!'

Just how much was at stake started to dawn on Olivia. This wasn't just some TV tabloid news story. This could mean the greatest witch hunt since, well, witch hunts. What would people do if they found out that vampires were living amongst them?

'We really need to get Serena Star off our trail,' Sophia said.

Ivy and Olivia both nodded in agreement.

'What do you have in mind?' Ivy asked.

'I don't know!' Sophia said exasperatedly. 'That's why I dragged you two in here.'

Ivy sighed, and all three girls fell silent for a moment.

'We need a distraction,' Olivia mused eventually.

'Exactly,' Ivy agreed. 'My father thinks that Serena Star will forget about Franklin Grove the moment there's some fresh Hollywood gossip.'

'Great!' Sophia responded sarcastically. 'All one of us needs to do is start dating *Celebrity Magazine*'s Hottest Man of the Year.'

'Can I volunteer?' Olivia put in, trying to break the tension.

'I'm just saying,' Ivy snapped at Sophia, 'that we need to find a story that's more interesting to Serena than vampires.'

'OK,' Olivia said, 'everyone calm down. Maybe we can try to convince Serena that there are werewolves in Franklin Grove instead – or something stupid like that.'

Ivy and Sophia exchanged nervous glances.

Olivia blinked. 'Don't tell me there *are* werewolves in Franklin Grove?'

Ivy raised her eyebrows just as the bell for first period rang.

'Saved by the bell!' Sophia blurted. She and Ivy flew out of the bathroom, leaving Olivia with her mouth hanging open.

Chapter Two

After third period, Ivy was still trying to figure out what to do about Serena Star. She pulled open her locker and distractedly wedged her notebook into a crevice between a stray boot and a stack of books. The entire contents of her locker started trembling, and Ivy lunged forward just as an avalanche of stuff tumbled out. She was left clutching a lone rubber vampire bat from the All Hallows' Ball, with a pile of things she didn't even know she owned at her feet.

This is not a good sign, Ivy thought.

It took her forever to pick everything up and

cram it back inside. Finally, the only things left on the floor were two black boots. Ivy went to pick one of them up, but it wouldn't budge. She pushed it with a frustrated grunt.

'Hey!' a voice cried as the boot moved away.

Ivy pushed her locker door shut to find Sophia attached to the boots.

'Where have you been?' Sophia demanded.

'Tidying my locker,' Ivy answered sheepishly.

'Tidying your locker!' Sophia repeated incredulously. 'Well, while you were cleaning out your locker, Serena Star convinced Principal Whitehead to call a meeting with the staff of the *Scribe*!' The *Franklin Grove Scribe* was the school paper, where Ivy was senior writer and Sophia was a photographer.

'Why?' Ivy asked.

'I don't know,' Sophia answered. 'But it can't be good!'

'When's the meeting?'

Sophia looked at her watch with false nonchalance. 'Oh, you know . . . RIGHT NOW!' she replied, pushing Ivy along in front of her.

As they charged through the halls, Sophia whispered, 'You know we're the only vamps on staff.'

'That's why we have to get on Serena's good side,' Ivy responded, following her friend through the frosted-glass *Scribe* office door. She saw at once that they were the last to arrive; everyone else was already seated around the big editorial table. At the far end of the room stood Serena Star, with Principal Whitehead at her side.

She's so much shorter than she looks on TV, thought Ivy.

'Thank you for joining us,' Serena Star said with a flash of her brilliant smile as she shot a tiny glance over the girls' shoulders.

Ivy turned to find herself face-to-face with a WowTV camera lens. She hadn't noticed the cameraman squeezed into the corner by the door. For a moment, she felt as if she'd been turned to stone; she *hated* being in front of cameras, crowds, and tape recorders.

Camera or no camera, I have to charm Serena Star, she told herself. With a gulp, Ivy looked right at Serena and smiled as brightly as she could. 'As the senior writer of the *Franklin Grove Scribe*, allow me to say what an honour it is to meet a journalist of your, uh, standing, Miss Star. I'm sure we all have a great deal to learn from you.'

'Thank you,' said Serena Star, clearly flattered by the praise. She gestured to the boy sitting closest to her. 'This young man has just finished saying so himself.'

Toby Decker, one of the best reporters on staff, blushed slightly. His blond hair was combed neatly off his face, and he was dressed in a blue button-down shirt and a red power tie. Ivy thought he looked like he was running for office.

Sophia and Ivy grabbed two seats next to Camilla Edmunson, who was the paper's book reviewer.

Serena placed her palms on the table officiously. 'I called you here, fellow reporters, because I need your help.'

'We'll do whatever we can,' said Toby eagerly, and everyone nodded.

'Good,' said Serena. 'Because I'd like one of you to work with me on my nationally covered story about life here in Franklin Grove.'

A bunch of people gasped.

'You mean, be your assistant?' asked Will Kerrell, a seventh-grader who usually covered sports.

'Exactly,' Serena Star nodded. She paused to let the information sink in. 'I'm holding an audition, and the person who wins gets to be my assistant.'

'How exciting!' Principal Whitehead said approvingly.

What is she up to? Ivy wondered suspiciously.

Serena Star looked around the table with her wide eyes. 'To audition, you have to get out there and get me a quote about Garrick Stephens and his coffin.'

'What kind of quote?' asked Kelly Marlings, flipping open her spiral pad and furiously starting to take notes.

'Something juicy,' replied Serena Star. 'Something that will make the American public sit up and take notice. And the person who gets the best quote will get to help me, WowTV's Serena Star, with my story,' she finished, her eyes sparkling.

Ivy was beginning to see what Serena had in

mind. *She's using us to find out stuff no adult could*, she thought.

Ivy felt Sophia slip a piece of paper into her hand. She unfolded it beneath the table and glanced down to see one of her friend's hastily drawn bunny cartoons. Surrounded by a bunch of wide-eyed baby bunnies was a particularly thin bunny with enormous eyes, long hair, and a sparkly smile – Serena Star, obviously. Her speech balloon said, 'The first little bunny to give up their fur wins a rabbit coat!'

Ivy hid her smile. *Serena Star isn't the most ethical reporter*, she thought, *but she's not as dumb as I thought.*

Ivy cleared her throat. 'Does the quote have to be about Garrick Stephens' stunt at the cemetery?' she asked. 'I mean, that was just a lame practical joke, right?'

'I think there's more to the story,' Serena said

meaningfully, 'and a good reporter will find out what.'

So much for my attempt to derail her, Ivy thought.

Camilla raised her hand, looking a little bored. 'Does everyone need to get a quote? I mean, I'm more of a critic than a reporter.'

'Only those with investigative reporting experience need apply,' Serena answered.

Ivy saw Sophia grin at Camilla and whisper, 'Looks like you and me are off the hook!'

'Well, for those of you who do audition, I cannot imagine a greater opportunity than working with a journalist as respected as Serena Star,' Principal Whitehead said.

A snort of disdain erupted from Sophia. Ivy kicked her under the table, and her friend tried to make it seem like something had been caught in her throat. She descended into a dramatic coughing fit, shrugging at Ivy in a way that said, 'Oops.' Camilla was also suppressing giggles.

If Serena Star noticed, she didn't show it. She flashed her trademark smile at the staffers around the table. 'You have twenty-four hours to get your quotes. May the best reporter win!' she declared.

'Thank you, Miss Star,' Toby Decker said professionally. With that, the *Scribe* staff started to file out of the room, chattering about their high-profile assignment. Sophia started to leave too, but Ivy put a hand on her arm. They had to talk to Serena first.

'See you,' Camilla said to Ivy and Sophia and headed towards the door. Just before she reached it, though, Ivy saw her do a double-take and walk over to the cameraman.

'That's the Sign of the Cyborg!' Camilla said, pointing to a symbol on the guy's T-shirt.

'You're a Coal Knightley fan?' he responded.

Soon they were deep in conversation about Coal Knightley's books.

Meanwhile, Ivy and Sophia went over to talk to Serena. The reporter grabbed Ivy's hand and shook it. As she did, she peered down at Ivy's fingers. 'Interesting choice of nail polish,' she said, raising her other hand and signaling her cameraman to come closer. He was too busy talking to Camilla to notice, so Serena smiled at Ivy in a plastic way and waved her free hand more frantically. Finally she snapped, 'Martin!'

'Sorry!' Martin the cameraman said, rushing over as Camilla left the room.

Serena huffed and let go of Ivy's hand at last. She looked at her and Sophia intensely. 'You two must be friends with Garrick Stephens.'

Sophia scoffed, and Ivy elbowed her before she said something rash. 'Do you mean because we wear dark clothes?' Ivy asked innocently.

Serena Star nodded. 'Exactly.'

Ivy frowned. 'You mean you agree with stereotypes?'

'What?' Serena Star spluttered. 'No. Of course not.'

'Thank goodness,' Ivy said. 'Because Principal Whitehead always says that a great reporter is never swayed by prejudice.' She smiled at the principal over Serena Star's shoulder.

'That I do!' Principal Whitehead confirmed cheerfully.

'I couldn't agree more,' Serena said stiffly, glancing uncomfortably towards the camera. She changed the subject. 'So where do you kids hang out?'

'The mall,' Sophia told her with a shrug. 'The diner.'

'Which diner?' Serena Star asked immediately.

'We like the Meat and Greet,' Ivy replied.

'Is that the one that's decorated like a meat locker?' Serena Star said.

Uh-oh, thought Ivy. *She's digging, and soon she's going to hit a coffin.* 'Plus I love Mr Smoothie's,' Ivy lied.

'Me too,' Sophia chimed in quickly.

Serena Star paused. 'So you two don't know Garrick Stephens?'

Ivy and Sophia didn't say anything.

'And you don't know anything about him or his friends?' Serena pressed.

'Everyone calls them the Beasts,' Toby piped up from a few feet away. Ivy hadn't even realised he was still there.

Serena Star nodded at him encouragingly, and Toby went on. 'They're always playing practical jokes and things. A few weeks ago, they dragged me to a party at Ivy's house, even though they knew I wasn't invited.'

Ivy winced. Serena turned to look at her. 'You invited Garrick Stephens to a party?'

'Just a, you know, a Halloween party,' Ivy gulped. 'Lots of people were invited.'

'But not Toby, who you work with closely on the school paper?' Serena said pointedly.

Ivy shrugged helplessly.

Serena Star turned back to Toby. 'What else can you tell me about Garrick and his friends?'

'I think they're into heavy metal,' Toby said, 'although that might just be their T-shirts. And they're always saying weird things, like "bloodsucker" this and "bloodsucker" that.'

Ivy's mouth went dry.

'Bloodsucker?' Serena's eyes widened. 'Are you sure?'

'Yes,' Toby replied.

Serena looked at her cameraman. 'That's a

wrap,' she said. She didn't even thank Toby or anything. 'Looks like we have some investigating to do, Martin. Let's start by doing some undercover eating at this Meat and Greet Diner, where *certain elements* seem to hang out.' She looked at Ivy and Sophia meaningfully. Then she marched out of the room, her cameraman hurrying after her.

'Celebrities,' Toby shrugged at Ivy and Sophia by way of explanation. They smiled back at him awkwardly.

A few moments later, Ivy and Sophia were trudging down the hall towards the cafeteria.

'You've got to do something, Ivy,' Sophia said.

'*Me?*' Ivy cried. 'What about *you?*'

'I can't. I'm just a photographer,' Sophia said. 'You have to get that assistant job.'

Ivy knew her friend was right, but it wasn't going to be easy. 'I have a feeling Serena Star doesn't trust me very much.'

'You have to make her!' Sophia pleaded.

Ivy thought about it and pushed her hair out of her face. 'What I need to do is come up with a killer quote that is also completely misleading.'

'Hey, that's all Serena Star does every day,' Sophia said with an encouraging smile. 'And you're much smarter than she is.'

At that very moment, Serena Star rushed past with her cameraman in tow. 'Didn't the actor Hank Hogart call his wife a bloodsucker after their divorce?' the girls heard her say. 'Maybe there's a connection there!'

Sophia and Ivy looked at each other and then burst out laughing as they pushed through the cafeteria doors.

❧   🦇   ❧

As she walked into media studies class, Olivia was having a hard time not imagining an angry mob storming into school and carrying off her sister for the WowTV cameras. She absent-mindedly took her seat beside Camilla as the bell rang.

In strolled Mr Colton wearing dark sunglasses and his trademark short-sleeved Hawaiian shirt. 'Good afternoon, media moguls!' he sang, dramatically throwing his old leather briefcase on to his desk. 'Judging from all the TV cameras around here, I'd say it's quite a day for media studies at Franklin Grove.'

He scanned the class until his eyes rested on someone just behind Olivia.

'Mr Stephens, it's clear from your little performance at the cemetery that last month's journalism segment made quite an impression on you.' Olivia and Camilla both turned around to see Garrick sitting with the other Beasts at the table behind them, an ear-to-ear grin above his Interna 3 T-shirt. 'Maybe next time, you'll actually complete the assignment on time,' Mr Colton finished with his eyebrows raised.

Ouch, thought Olivia. She couldn't help feeling pleased as the smile fell right off Garrick's face.

Mr Colton dug in his briefcase and held up a sheaf of papers. 'Drum roll, please!'

Everyone started drumming on their desks with their fingertips. The thrumming got louder and louder, until Olivia and Camilla were slapping the table they shared with their hands.

'Introducing . . .' Mr Colton shouted over the din, 'the Film Assignment!' He held the papers over his head in a disco pose.

Everybody laughed.

'Your mission, should you choose to accept it,' Mr Colton said, darting around the room and passing an assignment sheet to each student, 'is to produce, film and edit a five-minute documentary.

'You can pick any topic you choose, as long as it's appropriate. That means,' he said, looking fierce, 'no footage of me dancing and singing *Do the Dudley* from my 1989 appearance on *Star Search*.'

After Mr Colton had explained the process for reserving cameras and time in the school's editing suite, he said, 'I know everyone's anxious to get started, so why don't you take a few minutes to talk in your groups about possible topics?'

Camilla turned to Olivia. 'So, what should we do?' she asked excitedly.

Olivia thought of Charlotte on the front steps this morning, directing her to talk about what it was like to be a new student in Franklin Grove. 'What about a documentary that shows what it's like to move to Franklin Grove?' Olivia suggested. 'It could be an introduction to the town and what it's really like.' *Not what it's really like*, she thought, *but close enough to fool people like*

Serena Star.

Camilla frowned. 'I think Serena Star has the "truth about Franklin Grove" angle covered right now.'

Olivia knew Camilla was right. It wasn't a very fun idea for a school project, anyhow: it was sort of like trying to make the most boring film possible about Franklin Grove.

'I know!' Camilla said. 'I've always wanted to do something about alien life forms. We could show organisms from all different star systems.'

'That sounds cool,' Olivia said, nodding. Then she sighed. 'But do you think our budget's big enough to cover shipping and handling of alien organisms?'

Camilla blushed. 'I guess alien life forms are reasonably hard to find.'

There was snickering behind them, and Olivia heard Garrick say, 'That's killer!'

Olivia had really had enough of Garrick Stephens for one day – after all, he was the one that had started all the trouble with Serena Star in the first place. She spun around. 'Can you goons keep it down, please?'

The Beasts hooted. 'You're just jealous because we have the best idea,' leered Garrick.

Camilla turned around too. 'I think it's fair to say we've all seen enough of you in front of the camera, Garrick,' she said coolly.

'Picture it,' Garrick said, putting his thumbs and forefingers together to form a square viewfinder. 'A documentary that shows how violence is an important part of the modern middle-school experience. We're going to film the football games and call it "Cheers for Fears"!'

'Yeah!' All the Beasts guffawed, high-fiving each other. Olivia glared at them.

'Hey,' Garrick said, his eyes suddenly lighting

up. '*You're* a cheerleader, aren't you, Olivia? Want to star in my movie? Now that I'm famous, I've got *connections*.'

'You wish,' Olivia told him, rolling her eyes and turning back around. 'Unbelievable,' she added quietly to Camilla. 'Garrick's time in the spotlight has actually made him even more obnoxious!'

'No kidding,' Camilla agreed.

Olivia tried to tune out the boys behind her. 'Are you coming to the football game after school?' she asked Camilla.

'I was planning to.'

'Why don't you come over to my house for dinner afterwards?' Olivia offered. 'I bet it'll be easier to come up with an idea for our film without all the *chatter*.' She gestured over her shoulder, only to hear Garrick say, 'I bet those would make a good *impression* on a cheerleader!'

She had no idea what he was talking about.

'I have to check with my mom,' Camilla said, 'but that sounds great.'

Behind them all the Beasts shouted, 'TOUCHDOWN!'

Mr Colton shot the boys a look, and they all piped down.

'Just promise me Garrick Stephens isn't going to pop out of a casserole at dinner,' Camilla joked.

Olivia grinned. 'With my mom's cooking,' she said, 'he'll be burnt to a crisp *way* before that.'

Chapter Three

After school, Ivy stalked the halls with her notebook, trying to find the right quote for Serena Star. It was clear that Serena wanted something Goth, so Ivy was hoping for some titbit that would seem really grave, but was actually absolutely harmless. She talked to a sixth-grader whose cousin had got a tattoo of a skull on her ankle, a janitor who swore that spilt black nail polish could not be removed from school floors using any known cleaning solutions or polish removers, and the librarian, who told her that books with black covers were taken out less often than those with colourful ones. None of it was what she needed.

She was trudging along feeling utterly hopeless when she spotted one of the Beasts, Ricky Slitherman, rush out of a side door. *No matter what I come up with*, Ivy thought angrily, *Garrick and his friends will still be flapping their coffin lids*. She decided to follow Ricky outside.

When she emerged into the sunlight, Ivy saw Ricky heading towards the football field. When she got over there, she discovered that the Devils were only fifteen yards from the opposing team's end zone. The bleachers were pulsing with cheering people. Ivy peeked underneath them, thinking that that was where the Beasts were most likely to lurk, but there was no one there.

She was just walking around to the front of the bleachers to scan the crowd when she caught sight of Olivia, cheering on the sidelines. Her sister was standing atop another girl's shoulders with her hands on her hips and her face aglow with a natural smile. Olivia pumped her fist in the air and did a flip off the girl's shoulders. Two spotters on the squad caught her, and the crowd went crazy.

Ivy couldn't help going wild with everyone else, clapping and hooting loudly for her sister. Olivia seriously sucked – there was no doubt that she was the best cheerleader on the squad. Especially when compared to Charlotte Brown, who looked desperate for attention beside her.

Charlotte's face was plastered with a smile and eyes so wide that she looked like a cartoon smiley face. She was jumping up and down like a rag doll, throwing little waves and winks high up into the crowd. Ivy shuddered. It was seriously embarrassing.

Apparently, Charlotte couldn't even bear to

turn her back on the crowd when the cheer called for her to spin around. She rushed her move, immediately refocusing her gaze high into the bleachers and tossing off another cloying wave.

Ivy followed Charlotte's gaze and saw . . . the Beasts, sitting by themselves in the top row of the bleachers. Dylan Soyle had a huge video camera hoisted on to his shoulder, and he was pointing it down at Charlotte, while Garrick whispered in his ear.

Ivy remembered that the people in media studies were making movies; the Beasts must be at work on their project.

What's their topic? Ivy wondered. *Extra-annoying cheerleaders?*

Without thinking, she marched to the top of the bleachers and stood in front of their camera, blocking its lens with the back of her notebook.

'Hey!' Dylan cried, pulling his face away from the eyepiece.

'Turn it off,' Ivy commanded icily.

'You're interfering with an important movie shoot!' Garrick Stephens said.

'Turn . . . it . . . off,' Ivy repeated, narrowing her eyes into a death squint.

There was a long silence before Dylan glumly put down the camera.

'What do you want?' whined Garrick.

'I want you to climb back in your coffins and stay there!' Ivy snapped. 'You're putting us all in danger.'

'It's just a video camera,' Kyle said. 'It's not like a, uh, wooden stake or anything.'

Ivy rolled her eyes. 'It's not *your camera* I'm worried about,' she snapped. 'It's Serena Star's. At this rate, she'll be on to the vampire community in no time. You idiots are digging all our graves.'

Garrick shook his head. 'You're so *misguided*, Vega,' he said condescendingly, using the same word Serena Star had used for him on the news. 'Serena Star's not interested in all of us. She's interested in *me*.'

'Yeah,' guffawed Ricky. 'I think she wants to be Garrick's personal donor.' All the boys laughed.

'Serena Star is more likely to eat you alive,' Ivy seethed. 'You guys better start watching what you say.'

'Can I help it if the bunny ladies love me?' Garrick shrugged. He gestured to the cheerleaders. 'For example, look at Charlotte Brown, the star of my movie.'

Ivy spun around to see Charlotte glaring at her and waving her hands. 'Get out of the way!' Ivy could imagine her screaming. 'You're blocking my close-up!'

Ivy turned back to face the Beasts, and found that Dylan was filming again. 'You want a wooden stake?' she said with disgust. 'Here!' She flung her pencil angrily at Garrick – who shrieked and threw up his arms to shield himself – then spun around and stalked away.

🦇   🦇   🦇

After the game, Olivia and Camilla sat on the school's front steps, waiting for Olivia's mom to pick them up. All the TV news vans were gone, and the setting sun cast an orange glow over everything.

'We *killed* them!' Camilla said happily. 'Forty-six to three must be a record. Could you believe it when their lineman ran into the wrong end zone? Maybe our film project should be about embarrassing sports defeats.'

Olivia grinned. 'I think the Willowton Badgers have had enough humiliation for one year, without us making a *movie* about how bad they are.'

Camilla laughed.

'Hey, didn't you get a new cat?' Olivia asked.

'You mean Captain Whiskers?' said Camilla.

Olivia nodded. 'Maybe we could do something about him? I could imagine a cool documentary about what the world's really like for a cat.'

'As far as I can tell,' Camilla said, 'it's mostly sleeping and scratching.'

'Sounds like my Uncle Morris,' Olivia joked.

At that moment, her mom pulled up. 'Hello, girls!' she called excitedly out of the window, as Camilla and Olivia grabbed their bags and dashed down the steps.

'Hi, Mrs Abbott,' Camilla said, climbing into the back of the car.

'Hey, Mom,' said Olivia, as she slid into the passenger seat.

Olivia's mom didn't drive away. Instead, she wiggled her fingers on the steering wheel, and looked at Olivia out of the corner of her eye. Suddenly, she held out her hand. 'Pinch me!' she said.

Olivia stared at her. 'Why?'

'Fine,' Olivia's mom said. 'I'll pinch myself.' She grabbed a piece of her arm between thumb and forefinger. 'Ouch!' she cried. Then she grinned. 'It's not a dream!' she squealed ecstatically.

'Mom,' Olivia said, feeling confused, 'what's going on?'

'My great-aunt Edna died!' her mom replied, clapping with delight.

Oh my gosh! Olivia thought in shock; she'd never even heard of a great-aunt Edna before. *My mother has lost her mind!* She glanced at Camilla, who looked even more confused than Olivia felt, then turned back and said,

'And you're *excited* about this?'

Her mom gave her a stern look. 'Who do you think I am?' she said. 'That morbid boy that Serena Star is investigating? Of course I'm not excited about the death of a relative. But my great-aunt Edna was one hundred and two! She led an extraordinary life, and I know that it would give her great joy to see me so excited about what she's left to me.'

'She left you something?' Olivia asked. 'You mean like an inheritance?'

Camilla stuck her head between the front seats. 'What was so extraordinary about Great-aunt Edna?' she asked.

Mrs Abbott gave Olivia a pointed look before turning to Camilla and saying, 'Thank you for asking, Camilla.' Then she shifted the car into gear and pulled away from the kerb.

'It's quite a story!' she went on as she drove.

'You see, Edna lived in New York City in the 1920s. She was a maid in the household of an Italian duke. The duke was in New York searching for an American wife among the city's high society. Have you girls ever heard of Napoleon Rochester?'

'Wasn't he super-rich?' Olivia asked.

'Yes,' Camilla said, eagerly.

Mrs Abbott nodded. 'The duke was engaged to one of Rochester's daughters. But then, much to the shock of New York society and the duke's own family, he suddenly broke off his engagement!'

'Why?' Olivia asked.

'Because,' said her mother, 'he was in love with someone else. Someone from more *humble* origins . . .'

'You mean Great-aunt Edna?' Olivia guessed.

Her mom nodded. 'She was only eighteen

years old when he whisked her off to Italy,' she said wistfully. 'She'd never been more than ten blocks from home before.'

'Wow!' Camilla murmured.

'The duke lavished gifts on her, and they lived happily ever after,' Mrs Abbott declared cheerfully.

Olivia was impressed. 'Did you ever meet her?' she asked.

'Only once,' her mom replied. 'When I was about seven and living in Florida, Edna and the duke were touring the Florida Keys and they came to visit Grandma and Grandpa.'

'What was she like?' Camilla asked.

'She was the most glamorous person I'd ever seen,' Olivia's mom replied. 'She had this sparkly jewelled necklace that she let me try on, and I pretended I was a princess. And they . . . well, it was clear how much the two of them adored each other.' The car came to a stoplight, and she turned to Olivia. 'And that,' her mom finished, 'is the story of your Great-aunt Edna!'

'She sounds amazing,' Olivia said. 'I'm sorry I never got to meet her.'

'Me too,' her mother told her. 'But at least she left me some things that will help us remember her.'

'So what did she leave you?' Olivia asked.

Mrs Abbott sniffed, and Olivia realised that her mom's eyes were welling up. 'The diamond and ruby necklace that she let me try on as a little girl.'

'No way!' Olivia gasped.

'There's more,' her mother smiled, wiping a tear from her cheek with the back of her hand. 'She left me a jewelled ostrich feather fan, and a jewellry box with a secret compartment full of love letters written by her and the duke.'

Olivia turned around to look at Camilla and saw that her friend's mouth was hanging open. 'Are you thinking what I'm thinking?' she asked.

'Uh huh,' Camilla grinned. 'Looks like our film project is an old-fashioned love story!'

Chapter Four

Olivia rushed downstairs on Tuesday morning, her hair still dripping from the shower. She bounded through the small kitchen and into the family room, where she was frantically searching for the remote control between the cushions of the couch when she heard a noise: *Whooooosssshhhh!*

Olivia stopped in her tracks and stood up. She scanned the room, but nothing seemed out of the ordinary. *Maybe someone flushed the toilet upstairs,* she thought, bending down to look for the remote control again –

Whooooooooosssssshhh! The noise was louder this time.

That sounds so close, Olivia thought, her heart beginning to race. *I think it's coming from right behind the couch!*

She grabbed a cushion and crept to the end of the couch, holding the pillow over her shoulder like a baseball bat. Ever so slowly, she peered around the edge of the sofa . . .

'Whoooooosssssshhhhh!' her father exhaled, and Olivia found herself staring at the soles of his bare feet.

Ew, she thought, relaxing again. Her dad was lying on the floor in his pajamas with his eyes closed. For a split second she thought maybe he was hurt, but then his right leg came up in slow motion, and he brought his left hand over to touch his big toe. He held the toe aloft, his ankle shaking slightly.

'Whoooooosss—'

'DAD!' Olivia yelled.

Her father jumped as if she'd thrown a bucket of iced water on him. 'What is it?' he cried.

'What are you *doing*?' Olivia demanded.

'I'm practising the Li Ching,' he answered matter-of-factly.

Olivia had never heard of the Li Ching, but her dad was always taking up obscure new martial arts. None of them ever made him any cooler or any less embarrassing. 'You scared me,' she said.

Her father raised his chin. 'He who masters the Li Ching can do scary things!'

Olivia rolled her eyes and said, 'Where's the remote?'

Her dad shrugged and glanced around the room. Then he said, 'Oh!' and reached into the pocket of his pajamas.

Olivia grabbed the remote from him and flipped straight to *The Morning Star*. On screen, Serena Star was standing in front of Franklin Grove Middle, talking into her microphone.

'Anonymous sources say Garrick Stephens, the Franklin Grove student who hijacked a dead man's funeral on Sunday –' a leering photo of Garrick appeared beside Serena Star's head –, 'is kingpin of the Beasts, a gang of bullies who constantly reference the occult,' Serena Star reported gravely.

'Serena Star was at your school?' Mr Abbott said curiously.

Olivia shushed him with a vigorous nod.

'Some students believe that Mr Stephens and his friends' strange behaviour,' continued Serena Star, 'may be symptomatic of a much larger problem. One that's nothing short of . . . GRIMARKABLE!' A graphic with the word

'GRIMARKABLE!' appeared beside her head.

What a ridiculous word! Olivia thought. She was shocked, though, when the graphic was replaced by Charlotte Brown's flushed face, over a caption that said, 'Charlotte Brown, Head Cheerleader'.

'I was in the girls' bathroom, re-applying gloss, when two Goth girls came in,' Charlotte said. Olivia shut her eyes with embarrassment. 'They were dressed from head to toe in black rags, and their nails were covered in black nail polish.' And then, 'They *growled* at me!' Charlotte finished.

'So you think it's a problem,' Serena Star's voice said off-screen, 'that so many Franklin Grove students are obsessed with darkness?'

'Totally!' Charlotte agreed.

'Interesting,' Olivia's dad murmured.

Serena Star reappeared on screen. 'It's clear

that a sinister, corrupting influence is alienating the good students, like Charlotte Brown, at this school.' Olivia rolled her eyes as Serena Star walked dramatically towards the camera, stopping only when her face filled the screen.

'America, where there's smoke, there's arson! Who is behind the dark forces strangling Franklin Grove? Young Garrick Stephens clearly isn't smart enough to be the real ringleader, so who is it?' Serena demanded. 'I, Serena Star, am determined to find out, because the Star of truth must shine!' she cried, thrusting her microphone into the air. Then, with sudden calm, she smiled and said, 'I'm Serena Star. Wake up, America!'

Olivia shut off the TV. Her father noticed the frown on her face and said, 'Don't worry about those Beast boys, Olivia. I'll teach you the Li Ching so you can protect yourself.'

Olivia groaned and walked into the kitchen.

She was staring into space, thinking about Serena Star and eating a yogurt, when something in the next room caught her eye: a sparkling feather was sticking out from the top shelf of the tall glass cabinet where her parents kept the good china.

Olivia realised that after she and Camilla had pored over Great-aunt Edna's priceless artefacts last night, her mom must have moved them all up there so that they wouldn't get damaged.

Without another cheerleader in the room to give her a boost, Olivia had to drag her chair over to reach the top shelf.

Leaving the ostrich fan where it was, she carefully carried the wooden box back to the kitchen and set it before her on the breakfast table. She still couldn't get over how beautiful it was. The box was made of gleaming cherry wood, delicately carved with a pattern of flowers and birds.

Olivia opened the lid and gazed at Great-aunt Edna's precious necklace, which lay glittering on the deep blue satin lining of the compartment. For some reason, that made her think of Garrick Stephens in his luxury Interna 3, but she wiped the thought from her mind.

Olivia carefully lifted out the sparkling necklace and set it aside. Then she pressed ever so gently on the bottom of the compartment, just as her mother had shown her. There was a soft *click*, and the false bottom sprang open to reveal a stack of yellowed letters beneath.

A half-hour later, Olivia was still sitting there, reading. The letters were *so* romantic. She folded one, and unfolded another. It read,

My Dear Duke,
    You know that it cannot be. We are of different worlds. Oh, how I wish we could be together, but I

dare not allow myself to imagine a future in your arms. How wonderful it would be to live together in a home of love and peace, to have a precious child — a babe with your handsome eyes . . . But I must not write of such dreams. How my head battles against my heart!

Please do not look at me when I bring this afternoon's tea. I do not think I could bear it!

With love and sadness, Edna

As she finished the letter, Olivia felt a tear roll down her cheek.

'I made you some toast,' her mother interrupted. Olivia hadn't even noticed her come into the kitchen.

Olivia quickly wiped her cheek with the back of her hand. 'Thanks,' she murmured.

Her mom sat down opposite her and slid the plate of toast across to Olivia. She studied

Olivia's face. 'So . . . how are the movie plans coming along?' she asked.

'Good,' Olivia replied quietly.

Her mother nodded. 'What's wrong, sweetie?' she asked gently.

Olivia felt as if there was a lump in her throat. 'Nothing,' she said, looking down at the plate. Her mom reached over and took her hand.

Olivia fought the urge to cry. 'I guess,' she gulped, 'the family connection with Great-aunt Edna has made me think, you know, about my own biological parents.'

Her mom sighed and nodded. 'It's healthy to want to know about your birth parents, sweetheart,' she replied softly. 'I only wish I had more to tell you about them.'

'I know,' Olivia said.

'I'd be happy to get the adoption file out again for you to look at,' her mom offered.

Olivia took a tissue from the box on the corner of the table and blew her nose. 'There's not much *to* look at,' she quavered, looking up at the ceiling tearily. 'It just says that someone dropped me off at the adoption agency anonymously.'

'With the note that had your name and date of birth on it,' her mom added. Then she smiled and squeezed Olivia's hand. 'You know I've always loved your name.'

'Don't forget the ring,' Olivia said, wiggling her finger and forcing a smile.

'And the ring,' her mom agreed, standing up and coming around the table to give Olivia a big hug. Olivia buried her face in her mom's shoulder.

'I love you so much, sweetie,' her mom whispered, and Olivia found herself feeling a tiny bit better. Then her mom glanced at the clock over the stove. 'The Mom Express is departing for school in fifteen minutes sharp,' she teased. 'And you still haven't done your hair.'

Olivia grinned in spite of her tears.

'Why don't you go finish getting ready, while I put away Edna's things?' Mrs Abbott suggested.

'Thanks, Mom,' Olivia said and padded upstairs to do her hair.

Twenty minutes later, Olivia was staring out of the car window as her mom drove her to school. Her mind continued to buzz with questions about her real parents: *who were they? Why'd they give us up? Were they in love, like Edna and the duke?*

Two blocks from school, Olivia noticed a black-clad person walking on the sidewalk up ahead. Even from the back, she could tell it was Ivy.

'I'll get out here,' Olivia blurted. She really wanted to talk to her sister, but there was no way she could risk her mom seeing Ivy up close in case she noticed the resemblance.

'Why?' her mom asked.

Olivia hesitated. 'For the fresh air . . .' she tried.

Much to her relief, her mom pulled over without asking any more questions. Olivia hugged her goodbye and got out of the car. She waited for her mom to drive away and then shouted, 'Ivy! Wait up!'

Ivy turned, her face set in a scowl, and kicked some dirt off her boot as she waited for Olivia to catch up.

'You don't look too happy,' Olivia observed.

'I'm not,' Ivy replied flatly.

'What's wrong?'

'I still don't have a quote for Serena Star,' Ivy explained. 'But never mind me. What's the matter with you?' Olivia looked at her quizzically, and Ivy said, 'Just because you always look sunny doesn't mean I can't tell when you're feeling cloudy.'

Olivia smiled, and she and her sister started walking together slowly.

'Camilla and I are doing a movie for media studies,' Olivia began.

'I saw the Beasts working on theirs,' Ivy nodded. 'Apparently, Garrick's going to make Charlotte Brown a star.'

'Yeah,' Olivia sighed. 'Well, Camilla and I are doing ours on this relative of my mom's who I never even knew about: her Great-aunt Edna. She just died recently and it turns out she left my mom her love letters, plus some other stuff. There's a ruby and diamond necklace you'd love.'

'Really?' Ivy said, her eyes lighting up. 'That sounds killer.'

'It is,' Olivia agreed.

'So what's wrong?'

Olivia sighed. 'Do you ever think about our real parents, Ivy?'

'Every time my father drives me crazy,' Ivy said, cracking a smile.

'I'm serious,' Olivia said. 'All this stuff about my Great-aunt Edna has really got me thinking – about our family and history and stuff. I mean, I love my mom and dad and I feel super-lucky that they adopted me, but I wish so badly that we knew something, *anything*, about our biological parents. Who knows? Maybe we have grand-parents somewhere, or aunts and uncles and cousins. We could have a whole big family we don't even know about!'

'I thought about our parents a lot when we first found each other,' Ivy said. 'I'm lucky that my dad's seriously great, and that now I have you. But I'd like to know more about where we came from.'

'Exactly,' Olivia agreed as they crossed the street in front of school. 'I mean, who wrote the notes when they put us up for adoption?'

Ivy stopped in her tracks. 'What notes?'

'You know,' Olivia clarified, 'the piece of paper they left with the baby's name and date of birth on it.'

'I didn't get a note,' Ivy said. Then she murmured, 'At least not that I know of.' She bit her lip thoughtfully as they resumed walking.

'So how did you find out about where you were born?' Olivia asked.

'My dad told me it was in the adoption file,' Ivy replied. 'But he never said anything about a note.'

'Well, you should ask him. Serena Star doesn't have to be the only person in Franklin Grove determined to discover the truth,' Olivia said.

'Thanks for reminding me,' Ivy winced. 'I only have until lunchtime to save all of vampirekind! But as soon as I get through with that, we'll dig up our parents together. OK?'

'Sounds like a plan,' said Olivia with a grin. 'Good luck getting your quote!'

Ivy was already hurrying up the steps ahead of her. 'I need it!' she called over her shoulder.

🦇   🦇   🦇

By the break before third period, Ivy was flitting around school like a bat that couldn't find its way out of a cave. Her sister came bouncing towards her, jacketless to reveal a pink long-sleeved T-shirt that had the word 'Yay!' printed on it in blue bubble letters.

'Hey!' Olivia said. 'Any luck?'

Ivy shook her head, feeling faintly sick.

Olivia's eyes widened. 'You mean you *still* haven't found a quote?'

Ivy ran a hand through her hair. 'It's not for lack of trying!' she wailed.

'OK,' Olivia nodded. 'That's OK. We'll think of something.' She scanned the hallways as Ivy bit her lip hopefully.

'I've got it!' Olivia announced after a moment.

'What? What is it?' Ivy asked eagerly.

'Mr Slipson,' Olivia told her.

Ivy followed her sister's gaze, and saw the school guidance counsellor, Mr Slipson, waving his arms wildly as he talked to Mrs Klinter, the computer science teacher, in front of his office. The buttons were nearly bursting off his shirt, and a tiny paisley bowtie hung under his enormous chin. 'It's outrageous!' Ivy heard him cry, his tiny eyeglasses nearly popping off his round face.

The corners of Ivy's mouth curled. Mr Slipson was always going off on bizarre tangents that made no sense, and he was constantly saying things that were completely alarming but had no basis in reality. He was utterly *perfect*.

Ivy threw her arms around Olivia. 'You are seriously the best twin sister I have ever had,' she said.

A few moments later, Ivy was in position next to the guidance counsellor. 'Excuse me,' she interrupted him. 'Mr Slipson?'

'Ms Vega!' Mr Slipson bellowed. 'I was just telling Mrs Klinter here about the problem with toilet brushes.' Mrs Klinter smiled weakly before fleeing down the hall as if her life depended on it.

'Yes,' Ivy said. 'Um, Mr Slipson, I wonder if I could talk to you about –'

'Of course you can talk to me. That's my job, I'm a listener!'

'Right. Well, I'd love your thoughts for a story that Serena Star is doing,' said Ivy.

'Serena Star!' Mr Slipson gasped in delight. 'Her "Hygiene of the Rich and Famous" exposé last year was riveting!'

🦇 🦇 🦇

An hour later, Ivy walked into the *Scribe* office with Sophia. This time, they were the first ones to arrive, except for Principal Whitehead and Serena Star herself.

'Good morning,' Ivy said as brightly as she could, taking the seat next to Serena.

'Good morning,' replied Serena Star. 'As the senior writer here, did you get your quote?'

Ivy leaned closer to Serena and whispered, 'Garrick Stephens is just the tip of the iceberg.'

Serena Star's wide eyes shone with excitement. 'Well, I can't wait to hear what you've learned,' she said approvingly.

Camilla came in and went over to the cameraman. 'This is that *Eighth Dimension* book I was telling you about,' Ivy heard her say as she handed him a dog-eared paperback.

'Thanks, Camilla,' the cameraman replied with an appreciative nod.

The rest of the staff filed in. Toby sat down on the other side of Serena, straightened his polka-dot tie, and folded his hands on the table in front of him.

He looks confident, thought Ivy, shifting uncomfortably in her seat.

'Let's get started,' announced Serena expectantly. 'Who wants to go first?'

Marnie Squingle raised her hand, and Serena Star pointed to her.

Marnie cleared her throat and read from her notebook. 'Justin Fairfax, a Franklin Grove Middle School eighth-grader who has gym class with Garrick Stephens, told me – and I quote – "Garrick Stephens has the worst BO ever. He smells like death."' Marnie lifted her face with a look of smug satisfaction.

'That's it?' said Serena.

'He smells *like death*,' Marnie nodded. 'Isn't that shocking?'

'No,' replied Serena, 'not really. Who's next?'

Rudy Preston waved his beefy arm in the air. He glanced at the piece of a paper in front of him, and then folded it up and put it in his pocket.

He must have memorised his quote, Ivy thought, impressed.

Rudy looked around the table and began. 'I want to be Serena Star's assistant because she is the most beautiful, intelligent, interesting reporter working today,' he said in a steady voice. 'I admire her courage, her sense of justice, and her perfect smile. I remember the first time I saw her on television. I was –'

'Time out,' Serena interrupted. 'Is any of this going to be about Garrick Stephens and his cult?'

Rudy's eyes crossed. 'I thought you just wanted the best quote.'

'Next,' Serena said dismissively. Rudy opened his mouth and shut it again, clearly not understanding where he'd gone wrong.

'Poor guy,' Sophia whispered in Ivy's ear.

Next was Will Kerrell. Nervous at the best of times, he glued his eyes to his notebook and read in a rushed monotone, 'Those Beasts are into heavy metal music, and everyone knows that if you play that stuff backwards it will make you eat the head off a bat, and then you'll run into the street screaming and your eyeballs will explode and your brains will go everywhere!'

'Who said that?' asked Serena.

'My cousin Charlie,' Will told her. 'He's in high school.'

'Well, he's absolutely right,' Serena said. 'Unfortunately, heavy metal is old news.'

At this rate, Ivy thought hopefully, *I just might get the assistant job*. She took a deep breath and raised her hand.

'Let's hear it,' invited Serena.

'My quote is from Franklin Grove's very concerned guidance counsellor, Mr Reginald Slipson,' Ivy said. 'Mr Slipson has long suspected that something is very wrong with students in Franklin Grove. According to him, this latest incident at the graveyard was a perfect example of the sinister problem that is threatening our community.'

'This sounds promising,' Serena murmured. Camilla and Sophia looked at Ivy encouragingly.

'Mr Slipson has done some digging into the school records,' Ivy continued, 'and he's noticed a disturbing pattern. It appears students aren't getting enough sleep at night. In fact, Franklin Grove has more students falling asleep in class than anywhere else in the nation!'

'Why?' asked Serena.

'Yes, why is that?' asked Principal Whitehead.

Ivy raised her eyebrows. 'I think you'll all be shocked by the answer,' she said. Then she paused for effect and cleared her throat. 'I quote Mr Slipson directly: "What, exactly, are these students doing when normal people are in bed? Horrible things. *Unnatural* things!"'

Serena Star's eyes were wider than Ivy had ever seen them. Ivy leaned back in her seat and shared a triumphant look with Sophia.

After a second, Serena said, 'Don't stop there.'

'What?' Ivy stammered.

'Tell us the rest of your quote. What kind of "unnatural" things?'

Ivy hesitated. She had really hoped that what

she'd read would be enough to do the trick.

'Go on!' Serena insisted, and Sophia looked at Ivy hopefully.

Ivy read Mr Slipson's quote in its entirety, her voice getting quieter and quieter as she went along. '"What, exactly, are these students doing when normal people are in bed? Horrible things. *Unnatural* things! Eating junk foods packed with additives, listening to portable music devices, surfing the internet, playing video games, watching satellite television beamed from the sky. This insomniac epidemic is destroying our youth!"'

Serena tapped her pink fingernails on the table. 'I liked the beginning,' she said, 'but then you lost me. Help me out here. Is the scoop that kids are staying up late?'

'Exactly,' Ivy agreed.

Serena nodded. 'I was afraid so.' Then she added, 'What a snooze.' Everyone laughed.

Ivy pressed her hands into the table. 'The truth is sometimes less sensational than we imagine, Miss Star.'

'I know,' Serena said. 'Isn't that the *worst*?'

Ivy closed her notebook, trying not to look defeated. She knew that her quote wasn't what Serena Star was hoping for, but maybe the beginning would be good enough to get her the assistant job. *Or at least*, Ivy thought doubtfully, *convince her that there's no deep, dark secret in Franklin Grove.*

Soon the only person left to try out was Toby. He pulled a leather briefcase up on to the table and said, 'Before I begin, allow me to thank you, Serena Star, for this extraordinary opportunity.' Then he opened the briefcase and pulled out a single piece of typed paper, as if he was about to present an opening argument before the Supreme Court.

'I owe my quote to the dental profession,' Toby began, stowing away his briefcase. 'And more specifically, to my dental hygienist, Ms Monica Messler.'

Serena was not looking impressed.

Next to dentistry, my quote might not seem so boring after all, Ivy thought, brightening.

'Allow me to explain,' Toby continued. 'I was at a dentist appointment yesterday afternoon, when a repeat of the morning edition of *The Morning Star* came on the television above my chair. Ms Messler, who was cleaning my teeth at the time, said that she recognised Garrick Stephens. He had recently come to the dentist's office.'

Suddenly, a dark and heavy feeling spread through Ivy's chest. She and Sophia exchanged worried glances as Toby said, 'Ms Messler said it was a very strange visit.'

Serena Star leaned forward, clearly interested now.

'I nearly choked on the suction tube trying to ask her more about it. Here is what she said . . .' Toby looked down at his sheet of paper. '"Garrick Stephens came into the office last Thursday. He wanted to know how much a set of vampire fangs would cost."'

Ivy felt her skin flush, and she thought she might faint. She closed her eyes, trying to make the dizziness go away, and felt Sophia grab her hand tightly underneath the table. Ivy opened her eyes to find Serena Star staring right at her. Ivy looked away quickly.

'"We all thought it was such a strange request,"' Toby said, continuing his quote, '"especially because he isn't even one of Dr Roth's patients."'

'What happened?' Serena pressed.

'Nothing,' Toby shrugged. 'The receptionist told him he'd have to talk to Dr Roth, who was seeing a patient at the time, so Garrick said he'd come back later – but he never did.'

Serena Star was on her feet. 'Did he say what the fangs were for?'

'No,' Toby replied.

'Is she – the dental assistant lady – is she willing to go on camera?'

Toby nodded. 'I think so.'

Serena Star's wide eyes went starry. 'I can see the on-screen graphic now,' she murmured, spreading her hands in the air like she was making words appear on an invisible TV screen. 'FANGTASTIC!'

Then she blinked, picked up her bag, and gestured to her cameraman. 'Principal Whitehead,' she said, barely looking his way, 'I'm taking Toby out of school for the rest of the day on fieldwork. Toby, let's go!'

'But who won the assistant job?' Marnie Squingle blurted.

'Who do you think?' Serena shot back. And, with that, she charged out of the door, closely followed by Toby Decker, grinning widely as he hurried to catch up.

Ivy was about to bury her face in her hands when she heard a blubbering noise. Rudy Preston had burst into tears.

🦇　　🦇　　🦇

'Don't blame yourself, Ivy,' Sophia said as they trudged down the hall. 'How could *anyone* compete with a quote like that?'

'I know,' Ivy said. 'But this is seriously bad news, Soph.' She looked around to make sure no one was listening. 'A vampire inquiring about a new set of fangs? What was Garrick thinking?'

'Probably that his mom would kill him if he let his own incisors grow,' Sophia said gloomily.

'But why would he go to a human dentist?' Ivy said, utterly exasperated.

'You know the answer to that,' Sophia said, rolling her eyes. 'There isn't a dentist in our community who would agree to do it!'

She was right, Ivy thought. Getting fangs made – or even not filing down your real ones for an extended period of time – violated the 1926 Bylaw of the Night: a vampire will never try, or conspire to try, to bite a human. The risk of getting caught was too great, not to mention the fact that it was incredibly evil.

'Anyway,' said Sophia, 'it's time for Plan B: damage control. We have to keep an eye on Toby, and on what he and Serena are finding out.'

'And how do you suggest we do that?' Ivy asked.

'I was sort of thinking that maybe you could become Toby's new best friend,' Sophia suggested.

'As if,' Ivy replied. 'Did you see that tie he was wearing today? I don't really think I'm his type.'

'Come on,' her friend teased. 'You'd look killer in polka dots.'

That gave Ivy an idea. '*I* might not be the right person,' she said, looking down the hall, 'but I think I know who is.'

Ivy hurried over to join her sister, who was opening her locker.

'Did you get the job?' Olivia asked hopefully.

Ivy shook her head, and Olivia's face fell.

'We lost to Garrick Stephens asking a dentist for a set of fake fangs,' Ivy admitted.

Olivia winced. 'That doesn't sound good. What are we going to do now?'

'I'm glad you asked,' Ivy said. 'We're going to make sure we know what Serena Star's finding out even before *she* does.'

'How?'

Ivy smiled. 'Well, Olivia, have I ever told you how seriously great you are at making friends?'

Olivia looked at her suspiciously. 'Why do I think you're buttering me up for something?'

'I'm not,' Ivy answered innocently. 'I just thought you might like to make Toby Decker the next new friend on your list.'

'Toby Decker?' Olivia repeated. 'I know him. He's in my math class. He's nice. A little boring, though.'

'Not any more,' said Ivy. 'Now he's bound to have some interesting stories to tell; he's Serena Star's new assistant in Franklin Grove.'

Olivia took this in. 'I'd better start befriending,' she said.

Chapter Five

After school, Olivia was warming up for cheerleading practice in the gym, trying to ignore both Charlotte Brown, who was chattering on obliviously beside her about how being on TV had completely changed her life, and Garrick Stephens, who was lounging on the bleachers with Kyle Glass and leering at all the cheerleaders as 'research' for his movie.

Suddenly, the gym door swung open and in marched Serena Star, followed by Toby Decker and her cameraman. Charlotte's friend Katie shrieked and whispered, 'But I'm having the worst hair day!'

'Hey, Serena!' Garrick Stephens sprang up from the bleachers and trotted over. He was still wearing the same Interna 3 T-shirt, which Olivia thought was starting to look crusty. 'I was wondering when you'd be back for more of me!'

Serena turned to Toby and said, 'Keep him away from me,' loud enough so that everyone could hear. Toby looked doubtfully at Garrick and went to stand near him while Serena went up to Charlotte.

'I need to talk to you,' Serena said.

'Of course!' Charlotte winked at Olivia smugly as Serena led her out of earshot.

I have to hear what they're saying! Olivia thought. She started doing huge jumping jacks, inching closer to where Charlotte and Serena were standing with every jump. Finally she heard Serena Star say, '. . . you have a big role in a film that Garrick Stephens is making?'

Charlotte flipped her hair and said, 'Not really, it's just –'

'It's called "Cheers for Fears",' Garrick interrupted, reappearing beside them as Toby scrambled to intercept him. 'It's going to be a blockbuster!'

Serena spun around to face Garrick and snapped, 'Don't you have a coffin to be in?' Then she looked over his shoulder at her new assistant. 'Toby, is there a problem?'

'No, Miss Star,' Toby answered sheepishly. 'I mean, yes, Miss Star. I mean, come on, Garrick.' He put his hand on Garrick's arm.

Garrick shook him off. 'Showbiz,' he scowled. 'One day you're the big story, and the next you're out on the street.' He glowered meaningfully at Serena Star and then stalked away.

Serena turned back to Charlotte and switched her smile back on. 'Have Garrick or his friends ever asked you to do anything strange?' she asked.

'Like what?' said Charlotte.

'Like sleep in a coffin? Or do anything with vampire fangs?'

Charlotte laughed. 'Oh, *that*!' and Olivia's jumping jacks skipped a jack. 'I thought you meant something serious. Those guys are always playing Dracula. It's *so* lame. They're all like, "I want to suck your blood," and, "I should bite that guy's neck."' Charlotte rolled her eyes. 'I mean, this is eighth grade. Isn't it time to stop playing dress-up?'

Serena nodded. 'All this vampire talk could be the start of something dangerous,' she said. 'Have you heard of any vicious animal attacks or gruesome murders taking place in Franklin Grove?'

Charlotte frowned, looking faintly alarmed. 'No, I can't . . . I mean, I don't remember . . .' she stammered.

Serena smiled reassuringly and changed the subject, but Olivia's stomach was churning. Serena Star was becoming obsessed with vampire obsessions, and the problem was that that fixation could well lead her to stumble on the truth.

Out of the corner of her eye, Olivia saw Garrick still lurking off to one side. He was clearly eavesdropping, just like she was, and he did not seem happy with Charlotte's description of the Beasts' behaviour. Olivia saw him gesture to Kyle Glass, and a moment later, the two boys slipped out of the gym.

Toby was still hanging around, waiting for Serena to finish talking to Charlotte, and Olivia suddenly remembered her promise to Ivy.

Now's my chance, she thought.

She did an extra-large jumping jack so that her arm accidentally clipped Toby's shoulder.

'Oops, sorry!' said Toby, stepping backwards apologetically.

Olivia gasped. 'Oh my gosh! Toby, I'm so sorry,' she said. 'Are you OK?'

He pushed a blond lock of hair off his forehead. 'Yes,' he said, blushing slightly. 'No problem.'

'So,' Olivia went on, 'what have you been up to lately, Toby?'

'I'm acting as special assistant to WowTV's Serena Star on her big story about Franklin Grove,' Toby told her.

'Wow! Really?' Olivia said with wide eyes.

'Yes,' Toby nodded proudly.

'Any big leads?' Olivia inquired.

Toby looked around to make sure no one was listening. 'Garrick Stephens asked my dentist's office for a set of vampire fangs, and Serena thinks it might be the big break we've been waiting for! She's absolutely determined to discover everything she can about the obsession with vampires in Franklin Grove.'

'You're kidding!' Olivia exclaimed with a grin. 'Vampires?' *Maybe if I can convince Toby that there's nothing to the vampire angle*, Olivia thought, *he'll convince Serena Star.*

Toby nodded, looking slightly uncomfortable.

'Come on, Toby,' Olivia said, rolling her eyes. 'Serena Star might as well be looking for *werewolves* – I mean, witches,' she added quickly, remembering Ivy and Sophia's ambiguity on the werewolf front. 'You don't think there's anything to it, do you?'

'Honestly?' whispered Toby, with a backwards glance towards Serena Star. 'I've known Garrick and those guys all my life, and they are pretty strange. But lots of kids have issues. My father says they're just looking for attention.' He shrugged. 'Nevertheless, I have to do what Serena Star says. This job is a stepping stone for me. In a few years, I could be the youngest network anchorman in television history.'

Olivia believed he could, too – Toby was nothing if not driven. Suddenly, she thought she heard Charlotte mention Ivy's name, a few feet away. From the look on Toby's face, she knew he'd heard it too. They exchanged glances and edged closer to Serena's conversation.

'She is like the darkest Goth of all. She's been wearing nothing but black since before kindergarten – I've even seen her wear black *socks*. Isn't that *gross*? I live next door to her house, and sometimes you can see her lurking behind these thick dark curtains. Not that I would ever spy or anything,' Charlotte giggled uncomfortably. 'Anyway, if there's anything bizarre happening in Franklin Grove, I'd bet my poms that she's behind it. Even Garrick and the Beasts listen to her!'

'And you say this girl's name is Ivy Vega?' confirmed Serena. Olivia bit her lip.

Charlotte shuddered. 'Just the sound of her name gives me the creeps! You should read some of the morbid propaganda she writes in the school paper.'

Serena held up a pink fingernail. 'You mean, this is the same Ivy who's on the school paper?'

Charlotte nodded disapprovingly. 'I ask you: what is happening to journalism in our schools today?'

Serena Star narrowed her eyes. 'I thought there was something odd about her.' Abruptly, she turned to Toby. 'Toby, I want you to follow Ivy Vega's every move, and then report back to me. I want to know every single place she goes, every single person she talks to, and every single thing she does.'

HAMILTON COLLEGE LIBRARY

Olivia looked on with dread as Toby said, 'Right away, Miss Star.' He turned and smiled at Olivia. 'I look forward to speaking with you again when I'm not working, Olivia.'

'You too, Toby,' Olivia quavered, as he hurried out of the gym.

I have to warn Ivy that she's under surveillance! thought Olivia in a panic. Suddenly, Ms Barnett, the gym teacher, appeared. 'What's going on in here? Ms Star, this is cheerleading practice, not journalism club. You can talk to my squad some other time. We've got some serious cheering to do!'

🦇   🦇   🦇

It was nearly 4:30 p.m. Ivy had stayed after school to do homework in the library, but she hadn't been able to concentrate because she couldn't stop worrying about Serena Star.

Now she was at her locker, packing up to go

HAMILTON COLLEGE LIBRARY

and meet Sophia at the Meat and Greet. As she slammed her locker door shut, she thought she saw someone dart into a nearby doorway. She stared for a long moment, but no one reappeared. In fact, the hallway was almost completely empty.

This Serena Star thing has made me seriously paranoid, she decided with a shake of her head. In the library, she'd even convinced herself that someone was peeking in at her through the window.

Ivy turned and began making her way down the hall. No matter how many times she told herself nothing was amiss, she couldn't shake the feeling that someone was following her. Slowly, the hallways started filling up as people finished their clubs and sports practices.

At the corner of the main hall, Ivy set her jaw and abruptly spun around. Twenty feet behind her, a person in a blue shirt slipped behind a tall girl wearing a basketball jersey. The girl obviously found this odd, because she stepped aside to reveal . . . Toby Decker!

'Can I help you?' the tall girl demanded, peering down at Toby, her hands on her hips. Toby nervously caught Ivy's eye and lunged to bury his face in a nearby water fountain.

Suddenly Olivia appeared at Ivy's side. 'I've been looking for you,' she said.

'Apparently you're not the only one,' replied Ivy. 'I think Toby Decker is following me.' She gestured towards the water fountain, where Toby was peering at them as water filled his mouth.

'That's what I need to tell you,' Olivia murmured in a low voice. 'Charlotte told Serena Star that you're like Queen of the Goths, and now Serena's commanded Toby to follow your every move.'

'What!' exclaimed Ivy.

'Shhh!' Olivia said and gestured for Ivy to start walking beside her. She spoke out of the side of her mouth. 'Act natural. Serena also thinks people here are obsessed with vampires.'

Ivy's heart skipped a beat, and she couldn't help glancing over her shoulder, only to see Toby snapping a huge telephoto lens on to a camera. She whipped her head back around. 'He's trying to take pictures of us!' she gulped.

'We shouldn't be seen together like this,' Olivia said.

Ivy agreed with a tiny nod and whispered, 'Meet me at the Meat and Greet in thirty.' They split off in different directions down the hall.

A half-hour later, Ivy walked into the Meat and Greet, and saw her sister sitting alone in a booth next to the one where they normally sat, tucked in the back. She glanced over her shoulder, and saw Toby lurking on the edge of the parking lot.

Ivy and Olivia exchanged knowing looks, and Ivy went to her usual booth. She sat so that she and her sister were back to back, separated only by the banquette. Ivy picked up a menu and pretended to study it.

'I can't have Toby on my tail all the time,' she said to her menu. 'What if he follows me to the BloodMart or something?'

From the booth behind her, Olivia loudly ordered some chocolate cake. Then Ivy heard her whisper, 'Maybe it's not so bad.'

'That's what they used to say about public hanging,' Ivy murmured, 'and they were wrong about that, too.'

'Think about it,' Olivia whispered over her shoulder. 'If Toby's following you all the time, you can control what he sees – he won't find anything interesting if you don't let him.'

Ivy thought about it. Her sister had a deadly point.

Sophia arrived, looking down at them with a seriously puzzled look on her face. 'Why are you two sitting in separate booths?'

'Serena Star assigned Toby Decker to spy on me,' Ivy seethed. 'Olivia can't be seen with me because she's a double agent.'

'Craziness,' Sophia said, scooting in across from Ivy. 'I just passed Toby on my way in.' Then she whispered, 'Hi, Olivia,' to the back of Olivia's head.

'Hi, Soph,' Olivia whispered back.

'Do you think my cell phone's tapped?' Ivy asked.

Sophia rolled her eyes. 'You're under investigation by Toby Decker, Ivy. Not the FBI.'

Ivy leaned forward. 'Olivia found out from

Toby that Serena's really focused on the vampire angle now.'

'Oh, no,' Sophia groaned, dropping her face in her hands.

'Pretty bad, huh?' Olivia called quietly from the next booth.

Ivy let out a sigh. 'Can we change the subject and talk about something that doesn't make me feel like biting my own neck?'

For a long time none of them said anything. Then Olivia said, 'Did Ivy tell you about my film project, Sophia?'

Sophia nodded. 'She said you got all this killer stuff from a dead great-aunt.'

'Who married a duke,' Olivia added. 'It's actually really romantic.'

'I wish I could come over and see everything,' Ivy said to her fork. 'That necklace sounds drop dead.'

She heard Olivia shift in her seat and say, 'I don't think my parents should see us together. What if they notice how alike we are?'

'You two *still* haven't told your parents?' Sophia asked. Ivy shrugged by way of a response. So far, Sophia was the only other person in the world who knew Ivy and Olivia were twin sisters.

Suddenly, Olivia stood up, walked to the diner window, and looked outside. Then she came back and slid into the seat next to Sophia. 'He's gone,' she said. 'I just saw his mom pick him up.'

'That's the first good news I've heard all day,' Ivy said with relief, as the waitress appeared and set down Olivia's cake. Ivy and Sophia both ordered burgers.

Olivia was looking thoughtful. 'I've been wondering how come one of us is a vampire and the other human,' she said once the waitress had gone. 'Is it possible for someone to be born human, and then get bitten and turned into a vampire?'

'It can happen,' Ivy admitted. 'But for a human to get turned *into* a vampire, she first has to get bitten *by* a vampire – and that hasn't happened in generations. Even then, it would rely on the person surviving the vampire's bite.'

'And that almost *never* happens,' Sophia put in. 'It's seriously a one in a thousand chance.'

'Anyway,' Ivy said, 'I know I was born a vampire.'

'How?' Olivia pressed.

'Because of her eyes,' Sophia answered matter-of-factly. 'Born vamps have unusual eye colouring. Trans-vamps don't.'

Olivia's eyes suddenly lit up like she'd had an idea. She held up her spoon. 'How about this? Maybe *I* was born a vampire too, but then I got cured!'

'Cured?' Ivy repeated. She and Sophia

exchanged a grin. 'Being a vamp isn't a disease, Olivia,' Ivy explained. 'It's not like it is on TV. It's not a curse.'

'It's who we are,' Sophia agreed. 'It's physical. It can't be undone.'

Olivia frowned. 'So I guess that means one of our parents must have been a vampire, and the other a human,' she mused. 'Have siblings like us ever happened before?'

Ivy and Sophia exchanged glances.

'Um,' Ivy began, not wanting to freak her sister out. 'Actually, there's quite a lot of folklore about that.'

'About us?' Olivia asked.

'About humans and vampires, you know, mating,' Sophia explained.

'Most people think it can't happen, or that . . .' Ivy hesitated and looked at Sophia for help.

'. . . or that a human and vampire's offspring

couldn't survive, or would have four heads, or something . . . strange . . . like that,' Sophia put in helpfully.

'Hardly anyone believes the monster thing any more,' Ivy added hurriedly, seeing a look of alarm on Olivia's face.

'But the legends still crop up,' Sophia pointed out.

'I know,' Ivy agreed. 'But it's like vampires telling their kids that babies are delivered by bats. *That* isn't true either.'

'Anyway,' Sophia said, 'a vampire and a human getting together in that way is forbidden.'

'What do you mean?' asked Olivia.

'The Second Law of the Night,' Sophia answered. 'A vampire is never to fall in love with a human.'

'Maybe our parents broke that rule, and that's why they put us up for adoption,' Ivy suggested.

Sophia considered this and then nodded. 'If the coffin fits . . .' she agreed.

'Isn't there some way we can find out for sure?' Olivia wondered.

Ivy thought for a second. 'Have you ever tried talking to your adoption agency?'

'My mom and dad tried to get more information from them a few years ago,' Olivia told her. 'The only thing in the file was a copy of that note I told you about this morning. Do you know anything about *your* adoption?'

Ivy shook her head. 'I know that I was left at a special vampire adoption agency that placed me with Charles Vega, bachelor. I know my name, where and when I was born, and that my parents wanted me to have the ring. End of story. Whenever I ask my dad about it, he just says –' she imitated his smooth baritone – "You must look to the future, my Ivy, not back to the past." '

Olivia and Sophia both chuckled.

'I used to think he was right,' Ivy said with a shrug. 'But now I feel like I *have* to know about my past.' Ivy heaved a great sigh. All at once, she'd made up her mind. 'I'm going to talk to someone at the vampire adoption agency.'

Olivia leaned forward. 'You can do that?'

'I can try,' Ivy said. 'If we were able to find each other, maybe we can find our biological parents, too!'

Chapter Six

J ust before seven on Wednesday morning, Ivy was already dressed for school in a jagged black skirt, a dark red top, and a black crocheted sweater. She hastily grabbed a bowl from the cupboard, dumped some Marshmallow Platelets in it, and pulled the milk from the fridge. She plunked it all down on the breakfast table and switched on the TV, just in time to catch the opening credits of *The Morning Star*, which consisted of Serena Star's squeaky clean face super-imposed on the Statue of Liberty.

'Today,' the announcer's voice said, 'Serena

Star digs deeper into what's wrong with Franklin Grove!'

What's she going to dig up today? Ivy thought nervously, but her curiosity was immediately thwarted by a commercial break. By the end of the third commercial, which featured a seriously annoying dancing bottle of detergent, she was squirming with impatience.

Finally, *The Morning Star* came back on, and Ivy cranked up the volume. Serena appeared to be lying in a dentist's chair, today wearing a camel-coloured skin-tight suede suit. Behind her stood a dental assistant in pink scrubs, smiling awkwardly. Serena sat up. 'Good morning, America. I'm Serena Star.

'Welcome back to my ongoing investigative report on Franklin Grove, where this past Sunday, a thirteen-year-old boy named Garrick Stephens climbed out of a coffin during a funeral. Since then, an alarming portrait of this town has come to light – and it's filled with darkness.' Serena raised her eyebrows meaningfully. 'There's only one word to describe today's story: FANGTASTIC!' The word appeared in huge letters beside her head, and Ivy rolled her eyes.

'This is Monica Messler, a dental hygienist here in Franklin Grove. Why don't you tell America, Miss Messler, what you just told me about Garrick Stephens?'

Monica Messler cleared her throat nervously. 'He was in here last week,' she said, 'inquiring about getting a set of fake vampire fangs.'

'Shocking!' cried Serena Star, her eyes wide. 'Did he say what he wanted these "vampire fangs" for?'

Monica Messler shook her head. 'I guess he's seen too many horror movies.'

123

'Or perhaps,' Serena said, looking into the camera meaningfully, 'he's obsessed with vampires. And it appears he's not the only one in Franklin Grove.' She turned back to her subject. 'Miss Messler, have any other strange young people – commonly known as Goths – been in here making unusual requests?'

'I don't think so,' Monica Messler replied.

'Are you sure?' pushed Serena Star. 'Not even a girl named Ivy Vega?'

At the mention of her own name, Ivy dropped her spoon. Serena Star was checking up on her on national TV!

'Well,' said Serena, knowingly, after Monica shook her head, 'I'm sure it's only a matter of time.'

Serena stood up from the dental chair and stepped toward the camera. 'America, I, Serena Star, have uncovered a secret society of mysterious families in this sleepy town. They wear black clothes and heavy make-up. They keep themselves to themselves, rarely mixing with normal people. Why? Because they hide a truly menacing secret, and fake vampire fangs barely scratch the surface!

'But I won't rest until I find out everything this vampiric cult is hiding.' She leaned forward. 'Because the Star of truth must sh–'

Ivy flipped off the TV set and stormed into the kitchen. She was clearing away her breakfast bowl, when her dad walked in with the newspaper.

'Good morning,' he said.

'As if!' Ivy snapped.

Her father put his newspaper down on the counter. 'You appear to be upset,' he said.

'Serena Star said my name on TV!' Ivy exclaimed.

Her dad raised an eyebrow. 'Why would she do that?'

'Because,' Ivy huffed, 'I'm a Goth member of a vampiric cult hiding a terrible secret!'

'Oh,' said her father. 'Is that all?'

'Dad!' Ivy cried. 'Serena Star's not going to let the story rest until she has every one of us staked and boxed!'

'Ivy, you worry too much,' her father sighed. 'The vampire community is aware that Serena Star is digging. I promise you, she won't find anything.'

'Aren't you the least bit upset that she's investigating your own daughter?' Ivy demanded.

'Well,' he began, a smile creeping across his face, 'I *would* prefer the journalist in question to have a bit more gravitas than Serena Star, admittedly.'

Ivy threw a washcloth at her father's head, but he caught it.

'Honestly, Ivy,' he said with a short laugh.

'Vampires have been hiding from the world since long before you were born. Coffin chasers like Serena Star come and go.'

The mention of her birth reminded Ivy about her conversation with Olivia. 'Maybe that's why my parents gave me up,' she remarked testily.

'What?' her father said, suddenly turning serious.

Ivy looked at her father carefully. 'Maybe my real parents gave me up because someone was on their trail,' she said slowly, 'trying to expose them as vampires.'

'That's ridiculous,' her dad said briskly.

'How do you know?' Ivy asked. 'Did they leave a note with the vamp adoption agency or something?'

Her dad threw his hands in the air. 'No, of course not.' He started rummaging around in the fridge.

'And you never found out *anything* about them?' Ivy pressed.

Her dad closed the fridge without taking anything out and turned back to Ivy. 'I received nothing but your name, your place and date of birth, and your ring.' He smiled and gave Ivy a hug. 'But no matter. You yourself are all that matters – not your parents. You must look to the future, my Ivy –'

'Not back to the past,' Ivy finished for him, rolling her eyes. 'You always say that!'

'I say it,' he said gently, 'because it is true.' And with that, he picked up his newspaper and walked out of the room.

But it's not true for me any more, Ivy thought as she leaned against the counter. *I want to know more – not just for my sake, but for my sister's.* She had no choice but to see what she could find out on her own.

❧   ❧   ❧

At the beginning of lunch period, Olivia bounced into the school's editing suite and sank on to a swivel chair in front of a button-packed console. She and Camilla had reserved the suite so that they could record the voice-over for their documentary. As she waited for her friend to arrive, Olivia pulled out the script they'd written and quietly started rehearsing her lines – she was going to play the young voice of her Great-aunt Edna.

'My dear duke,' she whispered.

Suddenly, the room's loudspeaker crackled to life. 'OLIVIA ABBOTT,' boomed a computerised voice. 'I COMMAND YOU TO TELL ME THE DEEP, DARK SECRET OF FRANKLIN GROVE!' Startled, Olivia leapt to her feet. 'OR ELSE!' the voice finished.

Olivia peered around, confused and a little

frightened. *What is this, some weird Serena Star interrogation tactic?* she wondered.

Suddenly, a slim door in the corner of the room flew open, and Camilla stuck her blonde curly head round it. 'Is this place neat or what?' she grinned. Behind her Olivia could see a tiny grey room with padded walls and a microphone hanging from the ceiling. Hers was the voice Olivia had heard.

Olivia flopped back into her chair. 'You scared the living daylights out of me!' she wailed.

'Sorry,' said Camilla mischievously. 'So –' she grabbed the script from Olivia's hand – 'have you figured out who's going to play the duke?'

'I asked Brendan Daniels, Ivy's boyfriend,' Olivia answered.

Camilla looked pleased. 'He's perfect.'

'Unfortunately,' Olivia went on, 'he can't do it. He has band practice right now.'

130

'Oh,' Camilla said disappointedly.

'Maybe we can grab someone else,' Olivia said, rising from her chair and sticking her head out into the hallway. There weren't many people around, but then she spotted her sister, trudging along, looking totally ticked off about something. Olivia caught her eye and waved her over.

'Hey,' Olivia said. 'What's wrong?'

'What's wrong,' growled Ivy in a low voice, 'is that I'm fed up with having that bloodhound Toby Decker on my trail! All I've wanted to do all morning is call the vamp adoption agency, but I can't do that with him watching me all the time.'

Olivia scanned the hallway over her sister's shoulder and spotted Toby peeking out from behind someone's open locker door. Today he was wearing a stripy tie. From a distance, he almost looked like an old-fashioned aristocrat instead of a slightly dorky eighth-grader.

'I have an idea,' Olivia sang, straightening her sparkly pink top and gently pushing past her sister.

Toby noticed Olivia approaching and stepped out from behind the locker door. He smoothed his hair back with his hand.

'Hi, Toby!' Olivia said. 'What are you up to?'

Toby blushed. 'Oh, you know. Nothing, really.'

Olivia widened her eyes and flashed Toby her biggest smile. 'That is so exactly what I was hoping you were going to say. Come on!' She linked her arm through his and started leading him towards the editing room.

'But –' Toby stammered, his eyes scanning the halls for Ivy.

'No buts!' Olivia said. 'You're just the man I need!'

'I am?' Toby croaked.

'You are,' Olivia nodded, giving his arm a

squeeze. 'Camilla and I are making a movie for media studies, and we've been looking *everywhere* for the right guy to play the dashing duke!' As she pushed Toby through the editing suite door, Olivia looked over her shoulder and winked at Ivy, who was lurking in a doorway across the hall.

🦇　🦇　🦇

'He was just perfect,' Olivia told her sister later that day. 'He's got a nice voice and he even put on an Italian accent. "Edna, bella,"' Olivia imitated, clutching her heart, ' "I cannot live without you." '

Ivy laughed so hard, black mascara tears streamed down her cheeks. 'Olivia,' she gasped, dabbing at them with the sleeve of her black crocheted sweater, 'you seriously suck.' Which Olivia knew was the biggest compliment a vampire could give.

'Don't I?' Olivia grinned.

'It was like being freed from prison,' Ivy said

giddily as the bell rang for the start of science class. 'I had the whole lunch period to myself! He did track me down again after English, though.'

'Did you book an appointment with the adoption agency?' Olivia asked hopefully.

Ivy nodded. 'I'm going after school.'

There was a flutter in Olivia's stomach. *Maybe today's the day I'll finally learn something about my parents*, she thought.

As Mr Strain started writing instructions for the day's chemistry experiment on the board, Ivy said, 'There's just one thing.' Olivia looked at her expectantly. 'I need you to help me lose Toby again.'

Olivia understood right away what her sister had in mind. It seemed like ages since she and Ivy had traded clothes and swapped places, but it was so much fun. A smile spread across her face.

'We'll switch!' they half-whispered together, as

if on cue – which promptly set them both off in another laughing fit.

'Ladies,' said Mr Strain sternly from the front of the room. 'Is there something humorous about oxygenation?'

'I'm sorry,' Ivy gulped, straining to keep from laughing. 'It's my medication.' Olivia clutched her chair to keep from falling off.

It took half the class before they could say anything to each other without automatically cracking up. Finally, as they were finishing their experiment, Ivy whispered, 'Where should we do it?'

'How about the mall?' Olivia suggested.

'Killer idea,' Ivy said. 'I'll head there with Toby in tow right after school. I'll go the long way.'

'And I'll take the short-cut,' Olivia said, blown away by how she and Ivy seemed able to read each other's minds, 'and wait for you in the girls' bathroom in the food court. Once we switch clothes, I can lead Toby around the mall while you go to your appointment.'

'Exactly,' said Ivy. Then added loudly, 'That's 570 millilitres.'

'Huh?' said Olivia, confused. Then she noticed Mr Strain standing right in front of their desk. 'Right,' she said, writing the number on their experiment log, '570 millilitres.'

As the teacher walked on to the next desk, Olivia felt Ivy slip something cool and metallic into her hand, and looked down to see that it was a set of keys. 'I'll meet you back at my house after a few hours,' Ivy whispered. 'Just walk in, say hello to my dad, and head straight to my room. Don't come out until I get there. Eventually, Toby will give up and go home.'

Olivia nodded. She'd have to call her mom and tell her that she was studying at someone's house.

She went over the rest of the plan in her mind, and the she started to grin again.

'What is it?' Ivy asked.

'If we're switching clothes, then you're going to have to wear *this* to the adoption agency,' she said, pointing to her pink sparkly top.

The look of complete horror on Ivy's face was more than Olivia could bear. She bust out laughing again, which set Ivy off, too.

'Ladies!' called Mr Strain.

Chapter Seven

Ivy had bats in her stomach as she strolled through the mall food court. She wasn't just nervous about her visit to the adoption agency; she was also excited about swapping identities with her sister. Switching was almost like being invisible. Especially this week, when she felt like a bug under a microscope. She couldn't wait to shed her skin.

She confirmed with a sidelong glance that Toby was still behind her as she headed into the ladies' room. *At least he can't follow me in here*, she thought. *Well, he could, but then he'd get arrested.*

There was no one in the ladies' room except an old woman bent close to the mirror, straining to put on pale lipstick with a shaky hand. *Where's Olivia?* thought Ivy.

The lady noticed Ivy and gingerly turned around, clutching her purse to her chest. 'You're one of those death children I heard about on *The Morning Star*!' she gasped.

Ivy put her hands on her hips. 'So?'

The lady wagged a bony finger. 'The Star of truth will shine!'

A stall door swung open and out marched Olivia. She walked right up to the old woman. 'Then you should be worried about all those stolen ketchup packets from the food court you have in that pocketbook,' she said, folding her arms disapprovingly.

The lady hurried out of the bathroom without another peep.

'Have a good day!' Ivy called after her with unGoth-like enthusiasm.

Five minutes later, Olivia and Ivy had changed into each other's clothes, and Ivy was putting the finishing touches to Olivia's black eyeliner. The spray-on whitener really made an enormous difference to Olivia's appearance.

'All right,' Ivy said, taking a step back to admire her work. 'You are now officially one of America's Most Wanted.'

Olivia laughed. 'And you should really consider wearing pink sparkles more often,' she responded.

They gave each other a huge hug.

'I hope you find what we're looking for,' Olivia said.

'Me too,' whispered Ivy. Then, with a playful wink, Olivia trudged out of the bathroom in Ivy's heavy black boots.

Ivy pulled her hair back into a ponytail and started putting on Olivia's shimmery pink lipstick. *It's pretty killer having a twin. Although*, she thought, reviewing her reflection in the mirror, *I always swore I'd never be caught dead in sparkles!*

🦇 🦇 🦇

Olivia looked through an on-sale rack of drab skirts in the back of Midnight Clothing. She never thought she'd ever feel this way, but she was sick of shopping. She'd led Toby around the mall three times already. Her feet, clad in Ivy's heavy black boots, were almost as sore as they were when she won the Cheer-a-Thon in sixth grade.

Right now, Olivia could see Toby lurking behind a pile of distressed black jeans. She glanced longingly towards the dressing rooms, wondering if she could hide out there for a while.

Toby would probably just camp out in the next changing room, she thought. She hoped Ivy was succeeding at the adoption agency, because this was starting to feel as bad as not being able to stick a round-off.

Suddenly, Olivia had an idea about how to liven things up. *It's time to find out just how far Toby is willing to go*, she thought mischievously. She turned on her heel and walked abruptly out of Midnight Clothing. After a moment, she heard a crash, and Olivia glanced over her shoulder to see that Toby had toppled a display of black sunglasses.

'Sorry!' he yelped to a store clerk as he hurried after Olivia.

Olivia walked briskly down the mall's main hallway. The hand-lettered sign in the window of Trudy's Beauty Palace couldn't have been more perfect: *WAXED LATELY?*

I bet he won't follow me in here! Olivia thought as she walked to the personal care section near the back of the store. She peered out from behind a pyramid of flesh-firming cream.

Toby was frozen outside in front of the *WAXED LATELY?* sign with a completely bewildered look on his face. He was hopping nervously from foot to foot.

He looks like he has to pee! Olivia thought with glee.

Toby craned his neck to see into the store, but Olivia ducked out of sight. Finally, she saw Toby take a pained breath and come inside.

Wow, thought Olivia. *He really is determined to get the inside scoop.*

A saleswoman in a white smock approached him immediately. 'Can I help you?' Olivia heard her ask.

Toby looked like a deer caught in headlights.

'Did your mother send you in for something?' the saleswoman persisted.

'No,' Toby finally managed. 'I'm just looking.'

Yes, but just how far will you look, Mr Dedicated Reporter? Olivia wondered, darting out of the store. In the next half hour, Olivia went into a bridal shop, a nail salon, and a bikini store. Toby gamely followed her into every one, no matter how much it clearly made him squirm. She was almost ready to admit defeat when she passed Panzer's Department Store.

Panzer's ladies underwear section was near the front of the store. Olivia grabbed the craziest thing she could find off the rack and carried it over to a floor-length mirror. In the mirror, she could see Toby pacing nervously near the front of the store, clearly trying to get up the courage to follow her.

Olivia held the garment up in front of her. It was a fake leopard-skin bra that was so pointy it looked like it was made of party hats. In the mirror, she could see the distant Toby turn fire-engine red. He threw his hands up in the air, walked out of the shop and sank down on the edge of the hallway fountain, his head in his hands.

A reporter defeated, Olivia thought. She did a little dance. 'I win!' she sang lightly. 'I win, I win, I win!' Then she noticed a saleslady staring at her like she had eighteen heads. 'Sorry,' Olivia whispered, putting the bra back on the rack and hot-footing it out of the store.

Olivia looked at Ivy's chunky black watch. *I think I've kept Toby occupied for long enough*, she thought, satisfied that she'd done a good job. It was time to head for Ivy's house.

After making her way through the food court and back across the main hall, Olivia could see the main doors out of the mall up ahead.

'Ivy!' someone called. 'Ivy!' the voice yelled

again. *They must mean me!* Olivia realised with a jolt and spun around.

In the distance, someone waved. A boy in black. Suddenly, Olivia's stomach filled with nervous butterflies as she recognised Ivy's boyfriend, Brendan Daniels.

'Hey,' Brendan called, his pale face breaking into a wide smile as he strolled up.

'Brendan,' Olivia said, glancing around nervously. Yep, Toby was still on her trail, lurking a few feet away. 'What are you doing here?'

'Just hanging out,' Brendan said. He threw an arm around her affectionately.

Fooling Toby is one thing, but I can't fool Ivy's boyfriend! Olivia thought. Brendan felt her stiffen and pulled his arm away. 'Ivy, what's wrong?'

Olivia blinked, her mind racing. *There couldn't be anything worse than Brendan realising I'm not Ivy right now*, she thought. *It could be the end of Ivy's relationship, and, with Toby Decker watching, maybe the out-ing of vampires!*

'Ivy?' Brendan pressed, looking a little worried now.

'Nothing,' Olivia said at last. 'I'm just . . . I told my dad I'd be home by 4:30, and I'm already seriously late.' She gave her best Ivy eye-roll.

'Perfect,' Brendan grinned. 'I'll walk you home. I need to get that English book I lent you so I can write my essay tonight.'

Olivia didn't move.

Brendan gallantly held up his arm for Ivy to take hold. 'Shall we?'

'Shall we what?' gulped Olivia.

Brendan frowned. 'Shall we go to your house and get the book?' he asked, looking puzzled.

Olivia let her hair fall in front of her face like Ivy sometimes did. 'Killer idea,' she croaked, taking his arm. *This was* so *not part of the plan!* she thought.

🦇   🦇   🦇

Ivy stood in front of the adoption agency, trying to get up the nerve to go inside. She didn't envy Olivia, who was at the mall being followed around by Toby, but she was still really nervous about her own mission.

The store's sign said *MILK DUDS*. It looked like a cutesy human baby store, but there was a tiny upside down 'V' in the corner of the window, so Ivy knew she was in the right place – places that served vampires often used a mark like that to identify themselves to their customers. If the agency was like most vampire businesses, it would be hidden at the back of the store.

In the storefront window, the reflection of Olivia's seriously embarrassing top floated beside an empty baby bassinet. Ivy felt her heart flapping in her chest. *This is where I might find out about my parents*, she thought. *What if I don't like what I find?*

Then she thought of how eager Olivia had been for her to come here. 'I hope you find what we're looking for,' her sister's voice whispered in her head.

Ivy took a deep breath, walked in, and headed straight for the back of the store, where she found a 'Staff Only' door in the crib section. Beside the door was a small metal plate that had a black button beneath a round speaker. Ivy pressed the button; somewhere, a buzzer sounded faintly. A moment later, the speaker clicked to life.

Ivy put her mouth close to it. 'Marmalade,' she said carefully. *At least it's better than the last password*, she thought. *I hate butterscotch.*

'Approach the mirror,' a nasal voice crackled.

Ivy looked around, and noticed that hanging on the wall nearby was a cartoon-ish ceramic monkey that had a round mirror where its face should be. She walked over, and the mirror slid down to reveal the pale, sharp face of a man with bifocal glasses. It was quite a head for a goofy monkey's body, and Ivy cracked a smile against her will.

The man scowled back. 'Can I help you?' he asked in a nasal monotone.

Ivy leaned forward and whispered, 'I'm here for the adoption agency appointment.'

The man peered over his glasses and took in Ivy's sparkly top. 'Did Serena Star send you?' he said suspiciously.

'No!' said Ivy. 'I'm – This is just my disguise. I wouldn't be caught dead in clothes like this normally.'

'Name?' he asked.

'Ivy Vega.'

The man pulled away from the mirror and looked down, presumably at the appointment book. He peered back up at Ivy, eyeing her top dubiously. 'Prove it.'

Ivy dug into Olivia's book bag, pulled out her student ID card, and handed it over.

The man barely looked at the card before passing it back. 'Looks fake.'

'It's not!' Ivy cried, but the monkey man just stared at her impassively. Ivy rolled her eyes. 'What do you want me to do, bite someone?'

'Very funny,' the man said, without a hint of a smile.

Ivy sighed with exasperation. Then she reached up and gently took out one of her contact lenses to reveal her natural bright violet eye colour. 'OK?' she demanded.

The man nodded grudgingly and Ivy heard a buzz come from the door. She rushed to put her contact lens back in and open the door before he changed his mind.

Inside, Ivy was surprised to find a medium-sized room packed with every conceivable item a vampire baby could want. There were utterly cute tiny black coffins lined up against one wall, and paper mobiles with bats and moons hanging from the ceiling. Ivy's heart nearly melted when she saw a little black babygro that said 'Got Blood?' on it.

'Can I help you?' asked a voice behind her.

Ivy turned to see a friendly looking woman whose pale face was punctuated by a shock of bright red lipstick. She was sitting at a desk with a sign that said *GIFT REGISTRY* and looking at Ivy expectantly.

Ivy walked over to her. 'I'm looking for the adoption agency,' she said.

'With a shirt like that,' the woman replied, 'I don't think any vamp in their right mind's gonna adopt you, honey!'

Ivy must have looked upset, because the woman added, 'Oh, I was just teasing. You must be Ivy Vega!'

Ivy nodded gratefully. At least she wasn't going to have to convince another person that she belonged here, in spite of her bunny outfit. 'But isn't this the gift registry?' she asked.

'Gift registry, adoption agency, it's all the same computer system,' the woman told her, knocking proudly on the flickering computer screen beside her. 'We just need clearance from the central office in Transylvania.' She handed over a clipboard. 'Now you fill out these forms, Ivy Vega, and we'll see if we can't take care of you.'

Ivy took a seat on a huge black rocking chair in the corner and started filling out the forms.

Name. Date of birth. Adoptive parent. Birth mother. Ivy stopped and looked up. 'What if I don't know the answer to something?' she asked.

'Just do the best you can, honey,' the woman said kindly.

A few minutes later, Ivy handed back the forms. The woman flipped through them quickly. 'Let me guess. You're looking for your mom and dad.'

Ivy nodded hopefully.

'Allrighty!' the woman said cheerfully, and Ivy had the un-Ivy-like urge to hug her. *It must be the sparkles*, she thought. *They've gone to my head!*

The lady picked up the phone and held it between one shoulder and her cheek, while she typed on her keyboard. 'Yessiree!' she chirped into the phone after a moment. 'Oh, that's good news, Vlad, good news!' She put her hand over the handset and told Ivy, 'I'm twenty-sixth in line to talk to an adoption supervisor in Transylvania!'

An hour and a half later, Ivy was still waiting. She'd overheard the woman behind the desk get approvals from no fewer than six different people in Transylvania, including one who had told her how to make a perfect haemoglobin soufflé.

Vampire bureaucracy is the worst! Ivy thought, slumped in the enormous rocking chair.

'Thanks again, Raj!' the woman said cheerily into the phone and finally hung up. 'Ivy Vega,' she said, 'I've got the necessary password and your answer's on its way!'

Ivy looked at her sceptically, but the woman said, 'I'm serious, honey, I have that little download progress thingie on my screen right now!'

Ivy leapt up, her heart suddenly racing. *This is it!* she thought. *I'm finally going to find out who they were!* Questions filled her mind as she paced the room: *Are they still alive? Did they love each other? Were they outcasts because of their love? Why did they give us up?*

The computer beeped loudly, and Ivy hurried over. 'What does it say?' she asked breathlessly.

The woman tapped a few keys, then some more, and then a strange look of confusion spread over her face. 'You sure your name's Ivy Vega?' she asked.

'Of course!' said Ivy.

'Well, honey, I'm sorry, but you're not in the system,' the woman said apologetically.

'What?' Ivy exclaimed.

'It says right here: "No record of an Ivy Vega."'

'That can't be right,' Ivy said, shaking her head emphatically. 'There must be some record of my dad adopting me. Did you look under Charles Vega?'

The woman typed in the name, and her

computer beeped again. 'No, honey, no available records of a Charles Vega adopting a baby in the last four hundred years.'

'No records, or no *available* records?' Ivy demanded. The woman stared at her blankly, and Ivy threw her arms in the air. 'I mean, vamps are so secretive, who knows what they're hiding over there in Transylvania?'

The woman sighed. 'I know this must be like waking up in the wrong box for you, honey,' she said, 'but there's nothing I can do.' She jotted something on a scrap of paper and handed it to Ivy. 'Here's the general email address for central inquiries. You're welcome to contact them yourself, and I'm sure you'll hear back within four to six months. But, trust me, honey,' the woman said with a shrug. 'You're just not in the system.'

Ivy was tempted to argue, but she knew it was useless. 'Thanks,' she said quietly, taking the email address and heading out the door. As she passed through the bunny baby store, she couldn't help thinking her father was right after all. 'Look to the future,' he always said, 'not back to the past.'

Especially because when I do look back, she thought, trudging into the street, *I can't seem to see a thing!*

Chapter Eight

Having looked everywhere else for Brendan's book, Olivia kicked aside a pile of black clothes and crouched down to peer under Ivy's bed. Pulling up the black velvet bed skirt, it took her a moment to realise the only thing under there was her sister's shiny coffin.

She bolted upright. 'Of course it's not under there,' she said, rolling her eyes like Ivy might. Brendan just looked at her, frowning. She couldn't tell whether he was amused, suspicious, or worried that his girlfriend had completely lost her mind.

Olivia peered around Ivy's room desperately. It was a complete mess – the floor was so littered with black shoes and clothes that she could barely see the carpet, the bed was a nest of bags, pillows, and cosmetics, and Ivy's desk looked like it had been hit by an avalanche of paper and CDs. Olivia had been looking for Brendan's book for twenty minutes already.

All she knew was she had to get him out of the house before Ivy came home. *He's bound to figure everything out if he sees two Ivys in one place*, she thought, *and that won't be good!*

It had been stressful enough getting to Ivy's basement bedroom in the first place. Olivia had had to try three different keys before she found the one that opened the front door, and then she'd had to stand there awkwardly while Brendan and Ivy's dad chatted amicably in the front hall.

160

Suddenly, Olivia spotted the corner of a book peeking out from underneath a grey towel on the floor. She dashed over, pulling the soggy towel aside to reveal a water-logged paperback.

Olivia had never felt so relieved to see a ruined book in her entire life. 'Oh, no,' she said, carrying the book over to Brendan, 'it got wet.' She held it out with an apologetic frown.

Brendan glanced down at the book. 'Ivy,' he said, 'this is from social studies. I need the English book I gave you last week.'

I am so dead, thought Olivia. She had to find Brendan's book fast, or he was going to realise something was up – if he hadn't already!

🦇   🦇   🦇

Ivy turned a corner and glanced forlornly up at her house, which loomed atop the hill at the end of the cul-de-sac. Right away, she saw that Toby Decker was lurking in front of

Charlotte Brown's house, right next door to her own.

Ivy dived behind an oak tree.

Peeking out carefully, she saw Toby walking along the curb as if it was a balance beam. He hopped off, looked up towards Ivy's house hopefully, and then hopped on again and teetered in the other direction.

Hasn't he given up yet? Ivy thought. Seriously, she'd had enough frustration for one afternoon. She was certainly in no mood to wander around the neighbourhood for all eternity, waiting for Toby Decker to call it a day.

Unfortunately, the alternatives were just as O-negative. If Toby spotted her going into the house dressed like Olivia, he might get suspicious. If Ivy could make herself look normal again, Toby might guess that he'd been following around an impostor all afternoon.

Worse, he might run and tell Serena Star that there were legions of identical Queens of the Damned roaming Franklin Grove.

This bites! Ivy thought, leaning back against the tree.

Charlotte was Ivy's neighbour on one side; on the other lived the Carltons. Their property ran up the length of the hill, to where a line of bushes separated the two yards. Ivy had no choice. It was risky, but she decided to try and sneak behind the Carlton's house, up the hill, through the bushes and into her own backyard. Then she could climb in her bedroom window without Toby seeing. There wouldn't be many trees to hide behind on the way, but luckily she had vampire speed on her side.

Ivy peeked out again. She held her breath, waiting for Toby to turn his back on her in his walk along the curb.

Wait . . . Wait . . . Go! she thought, sprinting out from behind the tree and dashing for the Carlton's backyard as fast as Olivia's pink mules could carry her. A weather vane planted in the grass spun wildly as she zipped past.

🦇   🦇   🦇

'You know what?' Olivia said desperately, tossing a tangled black skirt in the air. 'I'm really sorry, Brendan, but I don't know what I did with that book.' She pointed to her head. 'Cobwebs!' she sang manically. 'But I promise I'll keep looking and bring it to you tomorrow in school. OK?' Olivia glanced anxiously up the stairs toward the door. *Ivy's going to be here any second!* she thought.

Meanwhile, Brendan just kept staring at her with that same impenetrable look.

'OK?' Olivia pleaded again. 'I promised my dad I'd set the table for dinner, so you really, really have to go now.'

Without a word, Brendan started for the stairs. *He's finally leaving!* Olivia thought, nearly overcome with relief. Then he appeared to think better of it.

'Something's not right,' he muttered to himself.

He turned around at the bottom of the stairs. 'You've been acting weird since the moment I saw you in the mall,' he told her. 'The way you talk, the way you move . . . You're not acting like . . . like my girlfriend.' He looked at Olivia, his eyes filled with concern. 'Are you sure you're feeling OK, Ivy?'

Olivia gulped and nodded.

Suddenly, a totally horrified look spread across Brendan's face.

Olivia's heart stopped. *He's figured it out*, she thought. *Ivy is so going to kill me!*

'Are you *mad* at me about something?' Brendan asked shakily.

🦇   🦇   🦇

Olivia is not going to be happy, Ivy thought with a grimace as she stood panting at the back of her house. She'd run so fast that one of her sister's pink mules had shot off her foot like a rocket and flown way up in the air. Ivy didn't even know where it had landed. Still, she was seriously relieved to have successfully made it into her backyard without Toby seeing her.

Ivy hopped along the back of her house to her bedroom window, which sat at ground level. Kneeling down, she glimpsed her sister in the room below. *Good thing I left this window open this morning!* she thought. She got down on her belly and scooted through the window feet first.

'Hey, Olivia!' she called. 'I'm back!' As she felt for the landing with her feet, the other mule fell off and clattered down the stairs. She continued loudly, 'Toby Decker should be the one everyone's worried about. What a stalker!'

Olivia didn't answer.

'Olivia?' Ivy called. 'Olivia!' She found her footing, shut the window, and turned around.

Right away, Ivy noticed the panicked look on her sister's face, and she froze. For a moment, she couldn't figure out what was wrong. Then someone stepped out of the shadows. It was Brendan, staring up at her from beside the foot of the stairs.

Ivy watched her boyfriend look from her to Olivia and back again, a wrinkle of confusion spreading across his brow. *He just heard me call Olivia 'Olivia'! Ivy thought in panic. Several times! And she's supposed to be me!* As she stared at Brendan, she realised that it was time to tell him the truth, but her heart sank. *Once he finds out I've been keeping this a secret,* she thought, *he probably won't want to see me ever again!*

Chapter Nine

Olivia peeled her eyes away from her sister, who was frozen on the landing, and looked at Brendan, who was staring up at Ivy with his mouth hanging wide open. He looked even paler than usual.

'Bren,' Ivy said quietly at last, 'there's something I've been meaning to tell you.' She pulled her hair from its ponytail and descended the stairs to stand before him. 'Olivia and I are twin sisters,' she said, her voice trembling.

Brendan looked over at Olivia. 'You're not Ivy?' he asked.

Olivia shook her head.

'Whoa,' he said, and for a moment Olivia thought he might faint.

Ivy grabbed his hand to steady him, and Brendan's eyes flickered. 'That hand *feels* like you.'

Ivy smiled. 'That's because it *is* me,' she said quietly.

'You two . . . are *twins*?' Brendan stammered.

Ivy nodded. 'We only just found each other at the beginning of the school year,' she explained. 'I never even knew I had a twin sister before.'

At least we don't have to keep it a secret any more, Olivia thought.

'I have to sit down,' Brendan said drily. He pulled his hand from Ivy's and staggered to the corner of the bed.

Ivy followed, talking faster now. 'Not even the two of us noticed how much alike we look at first. But, apart from the fact that Olivia's a cheerleader, we're practically identical.'

Brendan shook his head. 'I don't understand,' he said. 'How come she doesn't look like a cheerleader right now?'

'Because,' Ivy said, wincing, 'we switched places.'

Brendan blinked slowly.

'Bren?' Ivy quavered. A single tear tracked down her face, and Olivia felt her own eyes well up. 'Are you OK?'

Brendan didn't answer.

Please, please don't break up with her, thought Olivia, biting her lip.

Brendan's voice erupted hoarsely at last. 'I . . . I just can't believe it . . . Long-lost twin sisters? It's like something from a book.'

Ivy took a deep breath. 'I'd understand if you never wanted to see me again, Brendan.' Her lip trembled violently. 'I should have told you. I *wanted* to —'

Brendan suddenly stood and put his hand on Ivy's face, gently wiping away a tear with his thumb. Ivy's spray-on tan rubbed off to reveal a pale stripe of skin. Brendan smiled and hugged her. 'I'm a bit confused, but I'm not mad,' he whispered, as Ivy wrapped her arms tightly around him.

Olivia wiped her eyes as she let out a heavy sigh of relief.

'There's something else,' Ivy sniffled, pulling back from Brendan after a moment.

'You mean you've got a secret bigger than your twin sister?' Brendan teased. Olivia chuckled nervously.

'Olivia and I aren't *completely* identical,' Ivy began. 'She's not a vampire.'

Brendan did a double-take. 'Ivy!' he whispered disapprovingly, shooting a quick sidelong glance at Olivia.

'I had to tell her, Brendan,' Ivy said.

Olivia stepped forward. 'I promised Ivy that I would never, ever tell anyone, and I won't, Brendan. I'll do anything to keep the vampire secret safe.' Brendan looked at her doubtfully. 'That's why I'm dressed up like Ivy right now – to keep Toby Decker off her trail.'

'What does Toby Decker have to do with anything?' Brendan asked.

'Serena Star has got him spying on me in the hope of finding out something sensational,' Ivy explained.

'Oh,' Brendan said. 'I guess that makes sense, then.' He chuckled. 'It's completely insane, but it does make sense.'

He and Ivy hugged again.

Olivia realised that her feet were killing her from marching around in Ivy's heavy black boots all afternoon. 'Hey, now that the big secret's out,' she interrupted, 'can we switch back?'

Ivy looked down at her pink sparkly top.
'Definitely.'

'Aw,' whined Brendan. 'But I really like you
in pink.'

'Really?' Olivia and Ivy both said in surprise.

'No,' Brendan answered mischievously. Then
he winked at Olivia. 'No offence.'

'None taken,' Olivia laughed as she and Ivy
headed for the black-lacquered screen in the
corner of the room to swap clothes.

Brendan started to laugh too. 'No wonder you
couldn't find my book!'

🦇   🦇   🦇

Ivy pulled her top over her head and came out
from behind the screen in the corner of the
room, leaving Olivia to finish changing.

Brendan's dark eyes lit up when he saw her.
'There you are,' he said, and Ivy's heart fluttered.

173

With a grin, she walked straight to her desk and pulled Brendan's English book from the middle of the heap. She walked over to him and held it out. 'Thanks, Brendan,' she said, and she wasn't just talking about the book he'd lent her.

Brendan brushed her hand as he took the book. 'You're welcome.' Then he added, 'No more secrets, though. OK?'

'OK,' Ivy said, pushing aside a shoe and some bags and sitting down beside him.

'You know,' Brendan remarked, 'you both do this thing where you scrunch your nose up when you're nervous.'

'My nose does not scrunch!' protested Ivy.

'Yes, it does,' Brendan smiled gently. He leaned back on his elbows. 'One vampire sister, and the other human,' he said, his black T-shirt stretching across his chest. 'That doesn't happen every day, huh?'

'No kidding,' said Ivy. 'That's why Olivia and I switched this afternoon. I went to the vampire adoption agency to see what I could find out about our parents.'

Olivia's head popped out from behind the screen, half of her face still covered with spray-on whitener. 'What did you find out?' she asked.

'Nothing,' Ivy shrugged. 'They didn't even have a record of my adoption. Apparently, no one named Charles Vega has adopted a child in the last 400 years! I think they must have lost my file.'

Olivia's face fell.

'I'm sorry, Olivia,' Ivy told her.

Olivia sighed. 'I've been spending so much time thinking about my mother and Great-aunt Edna and their history, you know, for this film project,' she quavered. 'I thought we might be able to get at least a clue into our *own* family.'

Ivy nodded sympathetically.

Olivia was silent for a moment, and Ivy couldn't tell if there was a tear falling down her sister's whitened cheek. 'I'll be done in a sec,' Olivia whispered at last, disappearing behind the screen again.

Brendan stood up abruptly. 'We should have a party!' he announced.

Ivy turned to him in disbelief. 'A party?'

'Sure,' Brendan nodded. 'Or have you and Olivia already celebrated the fact that you're long-lost twin sisters?'

Ivy shook her head, and Olivia's voice called from behind the screen, 'I could use a party!'

Brendan looked at Ivy. 'What do you say we go to my family's crypt? We'll bring some celebratory A-Neg for us, and we can pick up a fruit smoothie for Olivia on the way.'

Olivia emerged looking like herself again. 'What's a family crypt?'

'Lots of vamp families have their own tombs,' Ivy explained. 'It's sort of like our version of a vacation home.'

'My family's place really sucks, though,' said Brendan. 'I go there all the time just to hang out and play guitar. You'll dig it. Seriously.'

'I'm game,' Olivia grinned. 'My mom isn't expecting me home till 8:30.'

Ivy smiled. 'Then let's party,' she agreed.

'Does anyone else know you guys are twins?' Brendan asked.

'Well, there's Sophia,' Ivy replied. 'She figured it out weeks ago.'

'Then let's invite her too,' Brendan suggested. 'The more, the merrier.'

You are seriously the most amazing boyfriend ever, Ivy thought.

Olivia was bending down to put on the pink mule that was lying at the bottom of the stairs. 'Ivy, where's my other shoe?' she asked.

Suddenly, Ivy heard measured footsteps approaching from upstairs. 'My dad's coming!' she cried. 'He can't see the two of us together! Olivia, you have to go!'

Brendan whispered, 'You mean *your dad* doesn't even know?'

Ivy practically pushed her tottering, one-shoed sister up the stairs. When they reached the landing, Ivy hoisted the window open and helped Olivia tumble out through it. She slammed the window just in time to turn and see her father descending towards her.

'Hi, Dad,' she said, trying not to sound out of breath.

'Hello, Ivy,' her father replied.

'I was, uh, just coming up to tell you that

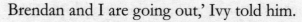

Brendan and I are going out,' Ivy told him.

Ivy's dad glanced past her to the bottom of the stairs. Brendan gave him a friendly wave.

'What a coincidence,' Ivy's dad said, and for a split second Ivy thought he knew something. 'I am also leaving, to go and inspect Mrs Wendell's new curtains.'

'Great,' said Ivy nervously. 'We'll follow you out.'

Her father peered into Ivy's eyes suspiciously. 'Ivy,' he said as Ivy's heart beat like a drum, 'have you finished your homework?'

Ivy blinked. 'Almost.'

'Then you'd best be back by 8:30 to finish it up,' her father said. 'Shall I pick you up something for dinner?'

'No, thanks, Dad. We'll grab a bite,' Ivy said.

Ivy and Brendan exchanged nervous looks as they followed her father back up the stairs, through the house, and out the front door. Then Ivy's dad kissed her on the forehead and got into his black convertible.

'That was close,' said Brendan as they watched the car head off down the driveway.

Then Ivy grabbed Brendan's hand and led him around the side of the house. They found Olivia, looking slightly dishevelled from having scrambled out of the window, staring up at a tall bush.

'Ivy, what is my shoe doing up there?' she asked, pointing to the mule, which was lodged on a branch near the top of the bush, like a pink bat.

As she followed Brendan, Ivy and Sophia into the oldest graveyard in Franklin Grove, Olivia glanced over her shoulder. She was still a little paranoid that Toby Decker might be following them, even though Brendan had done reconnaissance before they left Ivy's backyard. Brendan had said Toby wasn't lurking anywhere nearby, and they'd all agreed he must have finally given up and gone home.

Relax! she thought to herself, slurping her Strawberry Mango smoothie. As she gingerly stepped over a fallen tombstone, she was really glad they'd been able to get her other shoe down from that bush.

Deep in the centre of the cemetery, her friends stopped in front of a low, ancient-looking stone building that looked like it was sinking into the ground. A series of three arches supported by ivy-entwined pillars made an awning. Beneath the centre arch, Olivia could dimly make out a hulking stone door with tarnished bronze gargoyles on either side. In the middle of the door was an ornate square plate carved right into the stone, inscribed with a single word:

DANIELS. The letters almost seemed to glow.

'Ready for the underworld?' Brendan asked Olivia, who nodded nervously.

'Wait until you see the inside,' Ivy whispered.

Brendan ducked under the awning and turned one of the claws of the gargoyle on the right. There was a series of dull clicks and thuds, and suddenly the enormous door slid open. With a grin over his shoulder, Brendan stepped into the darkness inside.

Sophia followed right behind him, and Ivy went next.

Suddenly, Olivia realised her heart was thrashing like a pom pom. She wanted to walk into the darkness, she really did, but somehow it was just too *creepy*.

Ivy's head reappeared. She flashed Olivia a devilish grin, grabbed her hand, and pulled her inside.

Ivy led her through the pitch black and down a flight of uneven steps. Suddenly, Olivia heard the strike of a match, and a tiny flame illuminated the darkness. She saw that they were in some sort of antechamber, and it was *enormous*. It almost seemed impossible that such a big place could fit inside the structure she'd seen outside.

Brendan walked around, lighting a huge candle in each corner. Beneath the cathedral-like ceiling, the walls were covered with huge, strange markings carved deep into the stone, and the ground was grooved, as if a network of tiny rivers flowed through it. A small pointed tower of stone rose like a bony finger from the centre of the floor; a garland of long-dead flowers hung around it.

'This place is incredible,' Olivia stammered.

Each wall had an arch in its centre which led to another room.

'That room,' said Ivy, pointing to the passage on the left, 'is where all the urns of Brendan's relatives are.' Olivia peeked in to see dozens of ornate stone containers, each one on its own little shelf, rising from floor to ceiling. She was overpowered by a musty smell, and backed away.

Then Ivy gestured to the passage on the right. 'And that one his family uses for some of their more valuable antiques.' Olivia could dimly make out an elegant chaise longue, some gleaming candelabra and a big old wooden chest.

'But this one,' said Brendan, pointing to the middle room, 'has killer acoustics.' He ducked inside and started lighting more candles. The three girls followed.

The middle room was lined with a series of life-size bronze figures, sitting with their backs against the walls.

'Are there dead people inside those?' Olivia whispered.

Brendan shook his head with a little chuckle.

Brendan, Ivy and Sophia each took a seat on the laps of the effigies as Olivia stood in the centre of the room, looking around her in amazement and fascination. She loved the enormous tapestry silhouette of a huge leafless tree, which hung high up on one wall.

Finally, Olivia took a seat beside Sophia on one of the cool bronze laps. She leaned back. *This is surprisingly comfortable*, she thought.

Brendan opened his backpack and pulled out some plastic cups. Then he pulled out a dark bottle, uncorked it, and poured a round for himself, Sophia, and Ivy.

'Is that . . . you know . . .' Olivia stammered, desperately trying not to be lame. 'Blood?'

'Not really,' Sophia said.

'*Sophia!*' Ivy exclaimed, rolling her eyes.

'It's true!' Sophia cried. 'This stuff is packed with preservatives!'

Brendan raised his cup in the air. 'A toast,' he announced.

Ivy nodded. 'To family,' she said, looking right at Olivia.

'To friends,' said Sophia.

'To secrets,' Olivia said, grinning.

She soft-clinked her smoothie against her friends' cups, and a moment later, their laughter was echoing in the crypt's perfect acoustics.

Ivy hugged Sophia and Olivia goodbye outside the tomb. Brendan was staying behind to hang out and start working on his essay, and Olivia and Sophia had decided to walk home together, since they both lived in the same direction.

'Are you sure, Ivy?' Olivia asked. 'My parents

would never let me walk home alone after dark in a zillion years.'

Ivy smiled. 'I'm a vampire, remember? Night's my favourite time of day.' With a little wave, she set off across the graveyard.

Ivy stayed off the main streets, enjoying the darkness around her. She didn't have to be home for another half-hour, so she had lots of time. As she strolled, she couldn't help thinking about how happy she felt. It was strange, because in lots of ways, it had been a terrible day: from first thing this morning, when Serena Star had tried to implicate her on national TV, to her failed visit to the adoption agency. But, somehow, none of it mattered. Brendan was right: there was so much to celebrate.

He wasn't even mad, she thought tenderly.

Before she knew it, Ivy was climbing the long drive to her house. She glanced at her watch: 8:25, right on time. Her dad's car still wasn't back, though, so she reached into her bag for her keys. After a few seconds of rummaging, she realised she hadn't got them back from Olivia.

No big deal, she thought. She would just have to climb in through her bedroom window. Ivy calmly walked around to the back of the house, but was shocked to find that her window was closed. With a jolt, she remembered that she'd closed it after pushing Olivia out, so that her dad wouldn't catch them.

Ivy scanned the back of the house, and noticed that the window of her father's second-floor office was open. She smiled to herself. *I have to admit, being a vampire is pretty killer. After all*, she thought, taking a few steps back and peering around to make sure no one was watching, *it means I can do this.*

A super-huge leap landed her feet first on the

second-floor window ledge. Ivy deftly swung herself inside and shut the window. She wound her way down through the house, pausing in the kitchen to grab a cookie.

She stopped at the top of the stairs that led down into her room and surveyed the damage. *I didn't think it was possible*, she thought, smiling and shaking her head, *but Olivia has made my room even more of a mess!*

Chapter Ten

'Many think there is no deep, dark secret in Franklin Grove,' Serena Star was saying as the TV flickered to life in the family room. Olivia sank down on the couch, relieved that she hadn't missed the morning news. After last night's graveyard bash and then staying up late to do her homework, she'd overslept.

'They say,' Serena continued as the camera followed her down Main Street, 'that the Gothic culture here is no more harmful than football.' Olivia noticed that the camel suede suit Serena was wearing was the same one she'd worn yesterday. In fact, it sort of looked like she'd slept in it. Her make-up looked a bit hurried, too.

'And perhaps they are right,' Serena Star finished suddenly.

Really? Olivia perked up.

'I'd hoped to have the answers for you this morning, America, but –' Serena's face changed from serious to smiling – 'we were all shocked and overjoyed by last night's breaking news! That's right, I'm talking about Academy Award winner and former Miss America Charlene Costa's surprise wedding to country music heart-throb Manny Shucker. Tune in this afternoon for exclusive home video footage taken by the maid of honour, the final word on Franklin Grove, and other hot stories, on a special blockbuster edition of *The Morning Star*, later today!'

Serena Star flashed her trademark smile and

approached the camera. 'Because the Star of truth must shine! My name's Serena Star. Wake up, America!'

A smile spread across Olivia's face as she clicked off the TV. *Finally*, she thought as she headed upstairs to get ready for school, *the distraction we've been waiting for — Serena will probably be on the next plane to California to cover the Charlene Costa story!*

Ivy was walking down the hallway on her way to first period when she spotted the Beasts huddled together in a corner. There was something about them that wasn't quite right, but it took her a second to sink her fangs into what it was: none of them was laughing. *They're up to something grave*, she thought.

Charlotte Brown was passing by with her clique of bunny minions. Garrick lifted his head, and Ivy noticed that he was wearing the same Interna 3 T-shirt he'd been wearing all week. 'Charlotte!' he called. 'Wait up!' He separated from his friends and ran over to her.

Ivy slipped behind a school flag, hoping to catch a hint of what Garrick and Charlotte were talking about, but she couldn't hear what they were saying. She did notice Charlotte's bunny eyes light up, and saw her nodding like Garrick had just promised her a shopping spree. Then Charlotte ran back to her friends, Katie and Allison, shrieking, 'Guess what?' and Ivy heard them tittering excitedly as they disappeared down the hall together.

Garrick was slinking back to his friends with a devilish leer plastered on his face when Ivy intercepted him. 'What are you up to?' she demanded.

'Vega,' said Garrick. 'Wake up on the wrong

side of your box *again* this morning?'

Ivy narrowed her eyes. 'Don't you think it's time to wash your T-shirt?' she asked pointedly. 'It's ready to climb out of a coffin all on its own!'

'Hey,' Garrick retorted, 'I got a free top-of-the-line, brand-new Interna 3 out of all the publicity I've been throwing their way. And you thought jumping out of that coffin was a bad idea! Shows what *you* know.'

Ivy rolled her eyes. 'What's going on with you and Charlotte Brown?'

'None of your business,' he answered.

Ivy bore down on him with her death squint.

Garrick's mouth spread into a sinister grin. 'I'm, uh, *interviewing* her for my movie.' He raised his eyebrows and puffed out his chest. 'Once Serena Star sees it, she'll be *begging* me to come back on her show,' he added. 'And Charlotte might just win an Academy Award for Best Victim,' he finished with a wink.

Then he sauntered back to his friends, who greeted him with hoots and hollers, and Ivy frowned as she watched.

Suddenly, there was a tap on her shoulder, and Ivy turned to find Serena Star smiling at her strangely. Right away, Ivy noticed that there was something different about her. For one thing, her cameraman wasn't with her. Also, she was wearing the same suit she'd been wearing yesterday, and her hair looked unusually flat.

'I've been looking for you everywhere,' said Serena.

Ivy wanted to say, 'You mean Toby has,' but she thought better of it. 'Well, here I am,' she shrugged. 'Aren't you leaving for Hollywood to interview Charlene Costa?'

'Not until I'm finished with Franklin Grove,'

replied Serena, her eyes flashing. 'I thought you'd like to know that I've decided to reshape my story.'

Ivy took a step back. 'What do you mean?'

'Well,' Serena said, nodding wildly, 'I've been in this town all week, and it's clear that there's no big secret here.'

Ivy stared at her incredulously.

'So what I'm going to do,' Serena went on, 'is profile a Goth who's really a *leader* in this community. Someone who all the others look up to, a real role model. I can't think of a better way to show America that Goths are nothing to be afraid of. And guess who I want to profile?' Serena raised her thin eyebrows.

Ivy swallowed. 'Me?'

Serena unleashed a smile that nearly blinded her. 'That's right.'

'You're serious?' Ivy asked suspiciously.

Serena nodded enthusiastically. 'Aren't I always?'

She's not kidding, Ivy thought. *I think we might have fooled her.*

'So?' Serena Star pressed. 'Ready for your close-up?'

'I don't really like being the centre of attention,' Ivy said. It was true. Just the thought of being on TV made her stomach hurt – she'd had a hard enough time pretending to be head of decorations at the All Hallows' Ball. 'I'm not even wearing the right clothes,' she added, gesturing to her old black cardigan and flared black pants.

'I won't take no for an answer,' Serena said, with a sparkly smile.

If this is what it takes to shut the coffin on Serena's interest in Franklin Grove once and for all, Ivy thought, *I'd better do it.*

She forced herself to smile too. 'Then I guess I have to say yes,' she told Serena.

'Maybe we can pull Edna's jewelled fan across the screen to reveal a map of Italy,' suggested Olivia.

Camilla nodded enthusiastically. 'That's a great idea.' They were in media studies, working on the storyboard for their movie. Mr Colton said they had to plan every single shot, to make sure they used up the whole five minutes.

Behind them, Olivia could hear Garrick and his friends whispering intensely. Olivia heard Garrick mutter, '. . . on eBay. They were a sick bargain!'

'Let me see!' one of the other boys whispered. There was some rustling, and then Olivia heard something clatter to the floor. She looked down.

Gross, she thought, making a face. *Dentures.*

They were all old and yellow and pointy.

Wait a sec, Olivia thought. *Those aren't just dentures!*

Garrick snatched the teeth off the floor and shoved them in his pocket. 'You guys are going to get us staked!' Olivia heard him hiss as he slid back into his seat.

So Garrick's finally got himself a set of fake fangs, Olivia thought, *but at least he's trying to keep them a secret. Maybe he's finally decided to give the public vampire routine a rest!*

🦇   🦇   🦇

The bell for the end of school rang, and Ivy put her hand on Olivia's open notebook just as her sister was about to close it. 'Play dead for a minute,' she said quietly. 'I need to talk.'

The other students in science class filed out of the room. Mr Strain finished cleaning the blackboard and looked at them expectantly.

'We're just going to stay here and talk about

tomorrow's experiment for a few minutes, if that's OK with you, Mr Strain,' Ivy said.

'Of course,' Mr Strain replied. 'I'm glad you girls are finally starting to take scientific exploration seriously.' He picked up a huge pile of papers from his desk, squeezed them into his briefcase, and walked out of the door, leaving Olivia and Ivy alone.

'What's up?' asked Olivia.

'Serena Star wants to interview me,' Ivy answered nervously.

'No way!' gasped Olivia. 'I thought she was backing off.'

'She is,' Ivy nodded. 'She says she wants to profile a Goth student who's a good role model.'

'Great!' Olivia declared. 'At last this whole deep, dark vampire secret thing seems to be blowing over.'

'I guess so,' Ivy sighed. 'Then again, I'm not

sure which I think is more painful: being found out and burnt at the stake, or being interviewed on national TV by Serena Star!' She felt like there were bats in her stomach every time she thought of the coming interview.

'Oh, please,' Olivia said, nudging Ivy's arm reassuringly. 'You'll be awesome. Anyway, there's something I wanted to tell you, too.'

'What?'

'In media studies today,' Olivia lowered her voice, 'Garrick Stephens accidentally dropped something on the floor.'

'Like his brain?' Ivy joked.

Olivia cracked a smile. 'Like he has one?' she joked back. Then she shook her head and looked serious. 'Fake fangs,' she told Ivy.

Ivy pursed her lips. 'Hmm, Garrick was acting seriously strange this morning about Charlotte Brown,' she admitted. 'He was talking about his

201

media studies project, and he made a comment about her winning a Best Victim Oscar.'

Olivia's eyes widened. 'You don't think he'd try to bite her, do you?' she whispered. 'He wouldn't be that stupid, would he?'

Ivy gave her a doubtful look. 'These *are* the Beasts we're talking about.'

'Come on,' Olivia said, shutting her notebook. 'Garrick's been pretty desperate to get back on TV, and something involving fake fangs and a cheerleader could certainly get him noticed. We'd better find Charlotte.'

'And fast,' Ivy agreed, grabbing her bag. They bolted out of the classroom and into the hallway. 'There hasn't been a case of a vampire biting a human in generations,' she told Olivia as they raced towards the front hall. 'If Garrick even tries to sink his fangs into Charlotte, he'll do exactly what we've been trying to avoid – reveal the existence of vampires!'

Ivy spotted Charlotte's blonde ponytail bouncing across the hallway, with Garrick Stephens' dark silhouette slouching after her.

Ivy and Olivia raced down the hallway after them, and Ivy peeked around the corner just in time to see Garrick duck into the media studies classroom. She and Olivia snuck up on either side of the classroom door and peered in through its glass window.

Inside, Dylan Soyle was fidgeting with the school video camera as Kyle Glass adjusted a big light and Ricky Slitherman manoeuvred a fuzzy sound boom into position, huge headphones on his ears. Charlotte was sitting on a chair in the centre of the room, illuminated by the spotlight. She was looking at herself in a pink plastic compact, putting on extra make-up and fluffing her hair. Ivy watched her cycle through a series of facial expressions: a fat smile, a sultry pout, a surprised open mouth. Then she blew herself a big kiss. *Well, she's sure doing her best to look juicy*, Ivy thought.

'Where's Garrick?' Olivia whispered.

Ivy scanned the room, and directed her sister's gaze to a darkened corner near the back. Garrick's hands were lifted in front of his face, like he was putting something in his mouth.

'Please tell me that's just bubblegum,' Olivia quavered.

'I'm afraid it's the fangs,' Ivy whispered.

They could see Garrick's lips bulging slightly as he shot a ghoulish close-mouthed smile at the other Beasts.

Just then, Dylan Soyle burst into a coughing fit. Ivy couldn't hear him through the door, but it was clear to her he was faking it. All at once, he recovered, and when he brought his hands away from his face, Ivy could see there was something in his mouth too.

Kyle and Ricky had their own suspicious bulges behind their lips. Garrick wasn't the only one with fangs – they all had them.

They're actually gearing up to bite Charlotte! Ivy thought incredulously. She glanced at Olivia and saw that her sister had turned white as a sheet.

Garrick took his place behind the camera, and Charlotte put her compact and make-up away in her bag. A moment later, Dylan pressed a button on the camera, and Garrick pointed a crooked finger at his star. Right on cue, Charlotte plastered a smile on her face.

The other boys crept along the sides of the room as Garrick looked through the viewfinder and called something out to Charlotte. Ivy could just make out enough to know it was a question; the interview had begun.

Charlotte took a deep breath, batted her eyelashes, and started to speak directly to the camera.

Garrick nodded encouragingly as the other Beasts closed in behind her. Between Charlotte's heavy make-up and exaggerated facial expressions – and the fact that Ivy couldn't hear a word she was saying – she looked exactly like the victim in an old silent vampire movie.

🦇　　　🦇　　　🦇

'We have to stop them!' Olivia croaked. The Beasts were licking their chops hungrily while Charlotte prattled on at the camera, completely oblivious.

'Yes,' Ivy agreed.

Olivia was trying not to hyperventilate. 'But there are four of them, and only two of us. Plus they're all vampires!' She gulped for air.

'I really, really want to make it to ninth grade, you know?'

Ivy squeezed her sister's hand. 'Olivia, I've been putting up with the Beasts my whole life. They're complete wimps! You and I can definitely take them,' she said confidently. 'On the count of three,' she went on, putting her hand on the doorknob, 'we're going in. One, two –'

'Wait!' Olivia grabbed her sister's hand. 'If anything happens . . . I want your dark red top.'

Ivy cracked a smile. 'Three!' She turned the knob and eased the door open, but an unexpected noise stopped them from going further. They peeked in to see Dylan Soyle coughing up a lung again.

'Stop coughing, Dylan!' Garrick hissed. 'You're ruining the . . . er . . . the shot!'

But Dylan just kept coughing. Finally, Charlotte spun around in her chair, her lip curled

Fangtastic!

in annoyance. 'Why don't you go get a drink or something?' she snapped.

That's when Olivia noticed that Dylan's mouth wasn't puffed out any more. *He took out his fangs!* she thought.

Suddenly, Dylan was heading for the door. Olivia and Ivy dived out of the way as he burst into the hallway. Looking like he was going to puke, he fled in the direction of the boys' room.

From where she was crouched on the other side of the doorway, Ivy grinned at Olivia and mouthed the words, 'COLD FEET!'

Now that the door was open, Olivia and Ivy could hear exactly what was going on inside.

'Go on, Charlotte,' Garrick said, motioning frantically from behind the camera. 'Don't stop!'

'So unprofessional,' Charlotte muttered under her breath and adjusted herself in her chair. 'Like I was saying –' she switched her smile back on –

'the life of a cheerleader is filled with ups and downs, tosses and turns. Just like a real cheer!'

Behind Charlotte's back, Ricky and Kyle looked like they were having a silent finger-pointing contest. Olivia grinned at Ivy across the doorway. *They can't figure out who should go first!* she thought gleefully.

Suddenly, Kyle cleared his throat loudly.

'What is it now?' Charlotte snapped.

'Nothing,' Kyle stammered. 'Uh, I'm just going to go see if Dylan's OK.' And just like that, he rushed out of the room without a backward glance.

'You'll never work in this town again!' Garrick shouted after him. Then he leered at Charlotte, clearly determined to salvage the situation. 'Please, contin–'

'Garrick?' said Ricky bashfully from behind Charlotte's chair. 'I'm not really hungry either.'

Charlotte looked like she was on the verge of throwing the biggest fit in middle-school history. 'Hungry!' She leapt up from her chair. 'I'm lighting up the silver screen, and all you boys can think about is food?'

Ricky mumbled an apology and shuffled out.

'Garrick Stephens,' Charlotte said, marching right up to him, 'this is all your fault!' She poked him in the chest angrily. 'I'm going to have to start all over again!'

Suddenly, Charlotte peered at Garrick's mouth suspiciously. 'Are you chewing gum during my movie debut?' she demanded incredulously. 'You spit that out!'

Garrick's sunken eyes dulled with defeat. He turned his back on Charlotte, and Olivia saw him spit his fangs out into his hand. 'Show business,' he muttered forlornly.

Thrusting the teeth back into his pocket,

Garrick gestured for his star to return to her seat. In a grim monotone, he said, 'Charlotte Brown, cheerleader, take two.'

'It's Head Cheerleader, you dork!' Charlotte corrected.

Olivia and Ivy snuck away down the hall, rushed into the science hall bathroom and burst into laughter.

'I should have known they wouldn't go through with it!' Ivy cried.

'I'd say Charlotte was the only one who drew blood in that room!' Olivia joked.

A moment later, Ivy glanced at her watch, and her smile melted away. 'Oh, no,' she grimaced. 'I'm supposed to meet Serena Star in the *Scribe* office for my interview in five minutes!' She glanced at herself nervously in the mirror.

'Don't worry,' Olivia said. 'You look great.' She straightened the shoulders of her sister's black sweater so it fell squarely over her black pants. 'If Charlotte can survive her interview with a vampire, I just know you'll survive yours with Serena Star!'

Chapter Eleven

Through the window in the *Scribe*'s office door, Ivy saw a set-up that made the Beast's movie shoot seem even more amateur. The staff table had been removed, and the room's ceiling had been transformed into a canopy of bright lights and hanging microphones. Atop a square of carpet taped to the linoleum floor were two plush leather chairs that faced each other, and beside each one was a small side table.

Ivy noticed that Camilla was there, talking with the cameraman. Beside them stood the largest TV camera Ivy had ever seen, aimed squarely at the two chairs. *Is that a camera or a diabolical weapon?* she thought nervously.

Serena Star spotted Ivy looking in through the window. She bounded over and pulled open the door. 'Come in,' she said with a strange smile.

Ivy noticed she'd developed dark bags under her eyes, and strands of her hair were sticking out at odd angles. Her lipstick was uneven, and Ivy thought she saw a stain on the lapel of yesterday's suit. *In the last day or so*, Ivy thought, *Serena has gone from being perfectly turned out to looking slightly unhinged.* Somehow, her eyes had now widened beyond the point of reason.

Camilla waved at Ivy from where she stood by the cameraman. 'You look really nice,' she said. 'Martin here was kind enough to let me sit in. Since I'm in media studies, I thought it would be neat to see how a live interview is done.'

'Live?' Ivy quaked. She looked at Serena.

'This is going to be on TV *right now*?'

Serena nodded. 'Anything could happen,' she sang, steering Ivy to the far chair. 'Martin, how much time do we have?'

'Two minutes,' the cameraman responded.

Ivy started seeing spots at the corner of her vision, but then she realised it was just Martin testing the lights. *It's grim enough being on camera*, Ivy thought. *Now I have to go on live TV?*

'She's looking pretty pale, Serena,' Martin said. 'Should I get some blush on her?'

'No!' Serena said quickly. 'She's *perfect*.'

Camilla's smile of encouragement couldn't keep Ivy's heart from beating wildly as Martin counted down from behind the camera with his hand. 'Five! Four! Three! Two!' He mouthed the word 'One' and pointed to Serena.

'I'm Serena Star, and this is a very, very special afternoon edition of *The Morning Star*,' Serena announced. 'In a few minutes, I'll show you exclusive footage of It-Girl Charlene Costa's secret wedding. But first, join me for the shocking final installment of my week-long investigative report into Franklin Grove – the town that some people are calling Franklin *Grave*. I think you'll agree it's nothing short of . . . TERRORFIC!' Ivy could just imagine the graphic with the word 'TERRORFIC!' that was appearing at that moment on TV sets across the nation.

'Meet Ivy Vega, a typical eighth-grader here.' The camera swung towards Ivy, who forced herself to smile. '*Or is she?*' Serena Star added meaningfully.

'Ivy,' Serena said, 'I understand you're a writer on the school paper. What got you into journalism?'

What a lame question! Ivy thought. 'Well, I've

always liked to write,' she said simply. She waited for the next question, but Serena wasn't looking at her. In fact, she didn't even seem to have heard Ivy's answer. She was busy exchanging looks with Martin the cameraman.

Ivy scrambled to fill the silence. 'I used to be a cheerleader,' she blurted. *For about three days*, she thought with a wince. 'But it wasn't really my thing. So . . . I joined the school paper.' Martin reached his arm in and carefully placed a big glass of water on the table beside Ivy's chair.

'Some water?' Serena Star offered brightly, springing back to life.

'No, thank you,' said Ivy.

'Aren't you thirsty?' Serena pressed.

Serena Star's an even worse interviewer than Garrick Stephens, Ivy thought. 'No, not really,' she replied.

Serena glared at her. 'I insist.'

With a shrug, Ivy picked up the glass of water

and took a tiny sip. Serena Star leaned forward expectantly.

Actually, the water felt good. Ivy hadn't even realised how dry her mouth was. She took a big swallow, and Serena looked like she was going to fall off her chair. *When did drinking water become such a big deal?* Ivy wondered.

Ivy put the glass back down on the table, ready for the next question. Serena sat back in her chair, looking disappointed. 'Um . . . what's your favourite of all the articles you've done?' she asked.

'I did a series of pieces on the history of Franklin Grove Middle School that won a special achievement award,' Ivy explained, but once again, Serena appeared to lose interest the moment Ivy started talking. 'Most people don't know this,' Ivy soldiered on, 'but in 1924, US President Calvin Coolidge accidentally dropped his favourite pocket watch in –'

'What's your favourite book?' Serena interrupted eagerly. Then, before Ivy could even answer, Serena pulled a fat volume out from beneath her chair. She held it up to the camera before shoving it into Ivy's hands. 'How about this one?'

Ivy looked at the book in her hands. *The Bible?*

Serena Star stared at her accusingly.

'Well, it's certainly a good book. In fact, it's *the* Good Book,' Ivy said at last, cracking a nervous smile.

Serena's shoulders fell.

Suddenly, Ivy began to put two and two together, and Serena's strange behaviour started to make sense. *A bible, a big glass of water. She's testing me to prove I'm a vampire!* Ivy realised. *This isn't an interview about a good role model. Serena Star's trying to expose me! I bet that glass was full of holy water, and Serena must have thought the Bible would set me on fire or something!* Of course, that religious stuff only worked in the movies, but who knew what else Serena had up her sleeve?

If she hits on something real, Ivy thought in a panic, *I'll be revealed as a vampire on national TV!*

'Did you see her show on celebrity underwear, when her made-up word was "INCROTCHIBLE"?' asked Olivia, who was waiting for Ivy on the steps in front of school with Sophia and Brendan.

'No,' Sophia said. She shook her head in disbelief. 'Serena Star has her own ridiculous language.'

'As a matter of fact,' said Brendan, leaning back on his elbows so his black button-down shirt hung open over his white top, 'that's what I ended up writing my English paper on.'

'You're kidding!' said Olivia.

Brendan raised his eyebrows. 'I'm going to call it, "The Stupidfying Words of Serena Star!"' he said, laughing.

Olivia and Sophia burst out laughing too. Then the front doors of the school opened, and Toby Decker emerged, his tie hanging undone around his neck.

Olivia waved and walked over to join him. 'Hey Toby,' she said. 'Is Serena Star's interview with Ivy over already?'

Toby shook his head. 'Still going,' he replied. 'I'm surprised you're not watching it.'

'What about you, Mr Special Assistant? Shouldn't you be in there?' Olivia said. 'Camilla got a special invitation from the cameraman, but I didn't think I'd be allowed.'

'You wouldn't have, but it's live TV.' Toby shrugged. 'You could have watched it in the library with everyone else.'

'I didn't realise it was live!' Olivia exclaimed.

'It is,' Toby sighed. 'The only reason I'm not in there is that . . . well, I quit my job as Serena's assistant.'

'You did?' Olivia was shocked.

Toby hesitated, as if he was trying to figure out whether he could confide in her. 'Olivia,' he said finally, 'I think Serena is having some sort of nervous breakdown.'

'What do you mean?'

'She's convinced there are *real* vampires in Franklin Grove,' Toby explained, 'and that Ivy is one of them.'

Olivia felt a wave of panic wash over her. 'Why would she think a ridiculous thing like that?' she asked nervously.

Toby looked at the ground guiltily. 'Olivia, I have a confession to make. I followed you, Sophia, Ivy, and Brendan to the graveyard last night.'

Olivia was speechless.

'I'm sorry, I hope you're not mad,' Toby pleaded. 'I called Serena Star from outside the cemetery. I figured she'd be interested, since she's so convinced that Goth culture is corrupting the youth of Franklin Grove. Not that I think *you're* corrupted,' he added quickly. 'Well, anyway, Serena went there and . . .' Toby's voice trailed off.

'*And?*' Olivia urged.

'And I had to go home for dinner. But earlier today Serena told me that she followed Ivy back to her house, and that then she saw –' Toby hesitated.

'What?' Olivia gulped. '*What* did Serena see?'

'It's silly.'

'Toby, what did she see?' Olivia begged, fighting the urge to give him a shake.

Toby sighed. 'She said that she saw Ivy jump

into a second-floor window in a single leap.'
Olivia put her hand to her mouth. 'Serena called
it a "display of super-human strength". Then she
went off on this wild train of thought about how
she thinks people in Franklin Grove aren't just
vampire-obsessed. She thinks they're *actual
vampires*,' Toby went on as Olivia's heart pounded
in her chest. 'Right now, Serena Star is on national
TV trying to prove that Ivy is a vampire. I tried to
tell her not to, but she's planned a whole bunch
of ridiculous tests, like making Ivy drink holy
water and eat garlic.'

Olivia's eyes darted over Toby's shoulder to
where Sophia and Brendan were sitting. She
wanted to scream. She wanted to wave her arms.
She was overcome with panic. She didn't think
she could talk to Toby for another second. *Ivy's in
real danger!* she thought.

'I didn't think it was right,' Toby said, 'so I quit.

I mean, Serena just crossed the –' A car horn beeped, and Toby sighed. 'I gotta go,' he said sadly. 'Thanks for listening, Olivia.'

As Toby walked off, Olivia raced over to Sophia and Brendan. 'Serena's trying to reveal Ivy on live TV!' she cried. 'We have to save her! Come on, come on!' She dragged them to their feet, and started sprinting up the school steps.

'Wait!' said Brendan. 'Let's go that way!' He pointed around the side of the school, and Olivia realised that it would be quicker. Brendan and Sophia were much faster than she was, even with Olivia running flat out. She followed them past classroom window after classroom window.

As they neared the outside of the *Scribe* office, Brendan and Sophia abruptly slowed, and Olivia almost ran into their backs. Together, the three of them closed in silently and crouched below an open window.

Olivia heard Serena Star's voice saying, 'How many hours do you sleep at night?'

Olivia peeped over the windowsill. Ivy and Serena were sitting opposite each other in leather chairs, surrounded by lights, a hulking camera panning back and forth between them. She saw Camilla in the corner, looking weirded out. As for Ivy, she was shifting around uncomfortably in her chair, and Olivia could tell she was totally freaked. Olivia had the urge to reach out and touch her shoulder, to comfort her. After all, Ivy's chair was only a few feet away.

Olivia sunk below the windowsill and glanced at Sophia's black tank top and dark pants. 'I have an idea,' she whispered. Brendan and Sophia looked at her eagerly. 'If Serena Star wants a vampire so bad,' Olivia said, 'why don't we give her one?'

Serena Star fixed Ivy with an intense gaze. 'Have you ever gone sunbathing?' she asked, and leaned forward, ready to pounce.

Ivy squirmed in her chair, unsure what to say. 'I –'

Suddenly there was a blood-curdling scream in the hallway, and Serena bolted to her feet. 'Something appears to be transpiring!' she announced. Martin the cameraman swung the camera around to follow her as she rushed across the room.

Serena flung open the door, and Ivy heard a panicked voice cry out, 'A vampire! He's trying to bite me!' from the corridor.

Serena pointed frantically at the camera. 'We're still live, right?' she shrieked. Martin nodded fearfully. Camilla stood behind him, looking puzzled.

Ivy craned her head, trying to see. *Is it Garrick?* she wondered.

Serena stuck her head out of the door, and then pulled it back in right away. 'They're coming!' she cried hysterically.

Suddenly a girl ran down the hall and paused outside the doorway.

It's Sophia! Ivy realised with a jolt, but for some reason, her friend was wearing Olivia's shirt.

Sophia spun around to look behind her, horror filling her eyes as if something awful was approaching. A deep, diabolical laugh rang out.

'No! Please *nooooo!*' Sophia shrieked.

Another figure appeared beside Sophia. A man wearing a black cape. *Brendan!* Ivy's heart swelled. He grabbed Sophia, and she leant backwards, exposing her neck dramatically. Brendan immediately bared his teeth and bent over to bite her.

'I knew it!' Serena whispered in amazement,

but Ivy saw Camilla and Martin exchange doubtful glances.

After a moment, Sophia let out a blood-curdling scream, struggled from the vampire's grasp, and fled, with Brendan in hot pursuit.

Serena Star stepped out into the hall after them, madly gesturing for the camera to follow. Camilla and Martin began trying to awkwardly manoeuvre the apparatus through the doorway.

Suddenly, Ivy felt a tug on her sleeve. She turned to see Olivia bent down beside her, her face whitened, her eyes lined with thick black eyeliner. She was wearing black pants and a black tank top.

'Switch!' Olivia whispered, pointing to Ivy's top and swiftly handing over her own. Glancing at the doorway, Ivy hurriedly peeled off her sweater. Olivia snatched it and pushed Ivy towards the window.

Ivy scrambled and dived for the ground. Above her, she heard Sophia say in a normal voice, 'Ooh, that tickles!'

Then Brendan said, 'Hi Mom! Hi Dad!'

Serena Star immediately interrupted, saying, 'And now for a brief commercial break!'

Ivy laughed softly to herself as she heard Brendan and Sophia running off down the corridor, shouting, 'I'm a vampire!' in laughing voices.

Sophia and Brendan had played their parts perfectly. With Camilla and the cameraman struggling to get the giant camera un-wedged from the doorway, Serena Star was trapped in the hall. Olivia arranged herself in Ivy's interview chair and tried to catch her breath. Out in the hall, she could hear Serena Star's annoyed voice now apologising to America.

'When the vampire and his "victim" collapsed in fits of giggles and then ran off together down the hallway, your eagle-eyed reporter quickly realised that this was nothing more than a fantastic charade – two disruptive students' attempt to obstruct the Star of truth!' Serena declared dramatically. 'However, nothing will divert me from the real story here. Let us return to Ivy Vega . . .'

The cameraman finally succeeded in pulling the camera free, and Serena Star stormed back to her chair looking furious.

'Let's not pretend any longer,' she huffed at the camera. 'I didn't ask Ivy Vega here, America, so that she could tell you about her extracurricular activities. I asked her here because I've discovered the dark secret at the heart of Franklin Grove, and it is worse than you could possibly imagine! An undead people lurk here. They stalk the land, terrifying the locals and sucking the blood from this community!' She dug under her neckline and pulled out a crucifix. 'I've taken to wearing this to protect myself. Yes, America, there are vampires living in Franklin Grove!' Serena's wide eyes were enormous. 'And this eighth-grader is the worst of them!'

'But I still haven't answered your question about sunbathing,' Olivia said.

Serena Star glowered at her, and Olivia knew at once that she had her fooled. 'You're a vampire,' Serena Star seethed. 'And I'm going to prove it.'

Out of the corner of her eye, Olivia saw the cameraman gaping at Serena like she'd lost her mind. Meanwhile, Serena was pulling a small zip-lock bag from the inside pocket of her jacket. 'This is raw garlic,' Serena

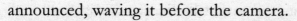

announced, waving it before the camera.

She held the clove out to Olivia with two fingers. 'Eat it!'

Olivia grimaced. 'No!' she exclaimed.

'*Eat it!*' Serena demanded.

'It will give me seriously bad breath,' Olivia protested.

Serena Star narrowed her eyes and turned to the camera. 'The fact that she won't eat it *proves* she's a vampire!'

Olivia sighed heavily and rolled her eyes. She took the garlic from Serena Star and lifted it to her mouth. Then she pretended to think better of it and shot a desperate look at the camera.

'Go on,' Serena sneered.

Olivia gave a dramatically fearful gulp before popping the clove in her mouth. Then she chewed with a pained look on her face, and the cameraman looked back and forth from her to

Serena Star anxiously. Finally, Olivia swallowed with great difficulty.

Her eyes began to tear, and she started to cough. Raw garlic was really strong!

Serena Star's wide eyes lit up in triumph as she pointed a manicured finger at Olivia. 'To dust, you blood-sucking beast!' she cried. She waved her arms at the camera. 'Watch now, America, as a single piece of raw garlic destroys this vampire so she can never threaten her fellow students again!'

Serena leapt to her feet. 'That's right! I, WowTV's Serena Star, have both broken the biggest story in history and saved humanity from the dark forces of evil!'

Serena turned, waiting for Olivia to turn to dust, but Olivia just stared back in mock horrified amazement. There was a very, very, *very* long pause.

'You stopped coughing,' Serena Star finally stammered.

'Duh,' murmured Camilla from the corner. Martin the cameraman buried his head in his hands.

'You can't fool me!' Serena Star snapped. She turned to the camera. 'I saw this girl leap on to a rooftop! She was in a graveyard! She *guzzles blood*!' she howled.

Olivia blinked and said, 'Are you OK?'

'I KNOW SHE'S A VAMPIRE!' Serena shouted.

Martin whispered something to Camilla. He stepped in front of the camera and took Serena Star's elbow, but she pulled it away and flapped her arm at Olivia hysterically. 'SHE'S THEIR *QUEEN*!'

'It's OK,' Martin said, firmly putting his arm around her. He looked into the camera grimly.

'This was Serena Star,' he said. 'Sorry, America.'

As Martin led her out of the door, Serena cried, 'Vampires are real!' and burst into tears. Olivia heard her sobbing the phrase over and over again as she was led away down the hall.

At last, Olivia turned to the camera and shrugged sadly. 'I guess the "Star of truth" shone too brightly,' she sighed. 'It seems to have burnt itself out!' And with that, Camilla shut off the camera and ended the interview.

Chapter Twelve

'Our thoughts are with Serena Star as we wish her a speedy recovery. This is Jack Donnell,' said the tanned former host of *Hollywood Hijinx*, who was filling in for Serena Star on Friday morning. 'Wake up, America!'

Ivy flipped off the TV and smiled at her dad across the breakfast table. 'Pretty killer story, huh?'

Her father looked at her proudly. 'You certainly made a finer impression than that boy Garrick Stephens.' He looked at his tea thoughtfully. 'The only element I still do not understand is how you were able to eat an entire clove of garlic without having a reaction.'

Ivy had already thought of how she'd respond if her dad asked that question. 'Dad,' she said coyly, 'you have to look to the future, not back to the past.'

Her father sat back in his chair. 'Does that mean you are not going to tell me?'

'Not unless you're going to help me find out about my adoption,' Ivy said.

With a tender look, her dad reached across the table for Ivy's hand – and promptly knocked over his cup of tea. He leapt to his feet, his grey wool chinos soaked. 'I have to change at once!' he said and darted from the room.

Ivy stared after him, wondering if he'd spilled his tea on purpose so he wouldn't have to talk about his least favourite subject.

After school on Friday, Olivia went to the Meat

and Greet diner with Ivy, Brendan, and Sophia to celebrate their victory over Serena Star. They grabbed Ivy's usual booth near the back, and soon enough Olivia was dramatically recounting the Toby Decker ladies' underwear incident. Brendan laughed so hard red lemonade went up his nose.

Suddenly, Olivia saw Camilla walk into the diner and look around. She waved and came over. 'Hey, everyone.'

'Hi, Camilla,' everyone replied, except Brendan, who was still laughing himself silly in the corner.

'Olivia,' Camilla said, 'I wanted to tell you I was finally able to book the video camera for –' She stopped mid-sentence, doing a double-take as she looked at Ivy and Olivia sitting beside each other. She blinked, shifting her eyes between their faces. 'Have you two ever noticed how similar you look?' she stammered.

Some secrets should stay hidden forever, Olivia thought. *But some really shouldn't.* She and Ivy shared a look, and Olivia knew her sister felt the same way. 'Camilla,' Olivia said, 'I think you'd better sit down.'

Sophia and Brendan obligingly slid over on their bench. 'It's like you're clones,' Camilla said excitedly as she sat. 'Or better yet, one of you travelled in time to meet yourself!'

Olivia laughed. 'No, you sci-fi nut, we're *twins*!'

'You're joking,' said Camilla. 'How can you be twins when you just moved here?'

Olivia shrugged, and Ivy said, 'Neither of us knew we had a sister until Olivia and I bumped into each other at school at the beginning of the year.'

'Are you sure?' Camilla said sceptically. 'I mean, apart from the fact that you look alike, how can you be sure you're actual twins?'

'Well, we both have the same birthday,' Olivia said.

'We were born in the same town,' Ivy put in.

'And we're both adopted,' Olivia added. 'Besides,' she went on, raising her hand as Ivy held up her necklace. 'Matching rings!' Ivy and Olivia said together.

'Left to us by our birth parents,' Olivia explained.

Camilla leaned forward to examine the rings. 'Wow!' she whispered.

'I just found out on Wednesday,' confided Brendan.

Camilla leaned back in her seat. After a moment, she said, 'I'm really disappointed you didn't tell me sooner, Olivia . . .'

Olivia started to apologise. 'I'm sorry, I –'

'. . . because we could definitely have got an

A plus with a movie called "The Long-Lost Twin Sisters of Franklin Grove!"' Camilla interrupted with a grin.

Olivia smiled. 'It'd be a really short movie. At least with my Great-aunt Edna's stuff there's some history to talk about. Ivy and I haven't been able to find out a thing about our background.'

Camilla was about to ask another question when, all of a sudden, Toby Decker appeared by their table, looking like his dog had just died.

'Hi, Toby,' said Olivia. 'What's the matter?'

'Everything,' Toby sighed. 'Now that Serena Star is getting "professional help", I don't even have a story to put in this edition of the *Scribe*.'

Olivia nodded sympathetically and turned to her sister. Ivy shrugged and gave a tiny nod, and Olivia knew they were both thinking the same thing. *More and more people are going to notice we look alike, and we're going to have to tell everyone eventually. Why not now?*

'Toby,' said Olivia, 'Ivy and I would like to give you the scoop of your career.'

Toby reached into his book bag and eagerly pulled out his reporter's pad. 'What is it?' he asked, squeezing into the booth beside her.

'Ivy and I are long-lost twin sisters who just found each other,' Olivia announced.

'Oh, no, you don't,' Toby protested, shaking his head. 'You can't fool me. If there is anything I've learned this week, it's not to believe outrageous stories with no basis in –' Suddenly Toby's jaw dropped, as he looked back and forth between Olivia and Ivy. 'You *are* twins!' he cried.

Ivy and Olivia grinned and nodded.

'First,' Toby said, scribbling on his pad, 'I want to know whether you have any early memories of each other.'

Ivy whispered to Olivia, 'Does this mean we both have to tell our parents now?'

Olivia scrunched up her nose and nodded. 'They probably should know before the whole school does.'

Ivy started to laugh, but then stopped abruptly. Olivia followed her gaze to the front of the diner.

Garrick Stephens was lurking by the door, wearing a different black T-shirt for the first time in days. The other three Beasts slouched in behind him, and they all started heading right for Olivia and Ivy's table. Olivia was steeling herself for a confrontation, but they stopped a few tables away, and Garrick looked down his nose at a couple of sixth-grade boys drinking milkshakes.

'This is our table,' Garrick hissed.

'Yeah,' guffawed Kyle, 'like we own it.'

One of the boys looked them up and down. 'It's a free country.'

Garrick leaned on his knuckles and sneered, 'You want to get bit?'

'Oooh,' said the other sixth-grader sarcastically, 'coffin boy is going to bite us. Help! Please! Oh, where is Serena Star when we need her?' The boy and his friend both cracked up.

Garrick straightened. He looked like he was trying to think of a comeback, except he wasn't smart enough. Finally he turned to the other Beasts and whimpered, 'I like sitting at the counter.'

'Yeah, we can spin the stools,' Dylan Soyle mumbled as the Beasts followed their leader to the other side of the diner.

'Some things never change,' Ivy laughed.

Olivia held up her glass, and her friends followed suit – except for Toby and Camilla, who held up salt and pepper shakers. 'To the Beasts,'

Olivia toasted. 'May their breath always be worse than their bite!'

Laughing, everyone clinked their glasses and shakers.

Ivy kept her glass raised aloft. 'And to secrets,' she said. 'There are those that should never see the light of day . . .' She smiled at Olivia tenderly, '. . . and others that need the sunlight to blossom.'

'Awww!' Camilla and Sophia both said.

Olivia's eyes welled with tears. She thrust her glass forward.

Clink! Clink! Clink! Clink! Clink! Clink!

Sink your teeth into
the third book starring
Olivia and Ivy

The secret is out – Olivia and Ivy are twins! But some
people are turning in their coffins about it. Ivy's adoptive
dad doesn't believe Olivia won't betray the Franklin
Grove vampires. To prove she can be trusted, Olivia must
pass three tests – but not just any old tests. These are
challenges to really get the blood pumping!

HAMILTON COLLEGE LIBRARY

Sink your teeth into the fourth book starring Olivia and Ivy

Ivy and Olivia have only been reunited for a few months and already they can't imagine life without each other. But Ivy's dad is moving to Europe – taking Ivy with him! Olivia and Ivy need to change his mind, but will the skills of two crafty twins be enough to stop a vampire from spreading his wings?

EGMONT PRESS: ETHICAL PUBLISHING

Egmont Press is about turning writers into successful authors and children into passionate readers – producing books that enrich and entertain. As a responsible children's publisher, we go even further, considering the world in which our consumers are growing up.

Safety First
Naturally, all of our books meet legal safety requirements. But we go further than this; every book with play value is tested to the highest standards – if it fails, it's back to the drawing-board.

Made Fairly
We are working to ensure that the workers involved in our supply chain – the people that make our books – are treated with fairness and respect.

Responsible Forestry
We are committed to ensuring all our papers come from environmentally and socially responsible forest sources.

**For more information, please visit our website at
www.egmont.co.uk/ethical**

Mixed Sources
Product group from well-managed
forests and other controlled sources
www.fsc.org   Cert no. TT-COC-002332
© 1996 Forest Stewardship Council

Egmont is passionate about helping to preserve the world's remaining ancient forests. We only use paper from legal and sustainable forest sources, so we know where every single tree comes from that goes into every paper that makes up every book.

This book is made from paper certified by the Forestry Stewardship Council (FSC), an organisation dedicated to promoting responsible management of forest resources. For more information on the FSC, please visit **www.fsc.org**. To learn more about Egmont's sustainable paper policy, please visit **www.egmont.co.uk/ethical**.